CLAIRE GETS CAUGHT

Claire allowed herself a moment of smugness. By the end of this day the group would have broken down into its component couples. Zoey would have found a place to be with Lucas, Aisha with Christopher, Nina with Benjamin. Only Claire and Jake would be wandering alone, unattached. But with a hot tub, a clear starry night, a fireplace, the warm, mellow afterglow of a day on the slopes . . .

It was a pity to have to manipulate him this way, but it was his own fault for being stubborn. She loved him, he loved her. Just because he seemed determined to screw that up didn't mean she had to let him.

There's a fabulous new MAKING OUT novel published every month!

MAKING OUT

Claire gets caught

KATHERINE APPLEGATE

Pan Books

For Fran Lebowitz and, as always, for Michael

Cover Photography by Jutta Klee

First published 1994 by Harper Paperbacks

This Pan edition published 1995 by Macmillan Children's Books
a division of Macmillan Publishers Ltd
Cavaye Place London SW10 9PG
and Basingstoke

Associated companies throughout the world

ISBN 0 330 34275 4

1 3 5 7 9 8 6 4 2

A CIP catalogue record for this book is available from
the British Library.

Printed and bound in Great Britain by
BPC Paperbacks Ltd

"This is it," Claire said. "This has to be the end. It's either me or Wade. One of us had to lose and . . ." She took a deep breath. ". . . He's already lost all he could."

"Claire—"

"No, don't, all right?" she said harshly. "This is hard enough. I really do care for you, and I know you care for me, so don't make me any sadder by saying it. There's just too much history between us. And to tell you the truth, I'm not a person who can go around for long feeling guilty. I'm sorry about what happened two years ago. I'm sorry you can't deal with this without trying to destroy yourself. But you can't. Which leaves only one solution."

His arms tightened around her, holding her close. She pressed her cheek against his shoulder and blotted her tears on his shirt.

He took her face with his hand and forced her to look at him. He kissed her for a long, still moment.

Then she took another deep breath. She let the emotion run out of her, turning her thoughts away. She thought of her widow's walk. She thought of

1

how much she liked to be up there, watching the lightning illuminate the darkness, watching snow drift down to settle on the little town below.

She had always been able to do what she had to. And now she pulled away, leaving the warmth of Jake's arms. She turned, and with dry eyes, walked away.

Claire left the dance, the sound of the music dying away behind her as she left the campus and headed down through the town, past the darkened storefronts and bright restaurants. It was a crisp, chilly evening and she walked briskly, her heels loud on the sidewalk.

It had gone pretty well, if she said so herself. Right now Jake was realizing what had happened: that she had given him up to avoid hurting him anymore. He was also realizing that he was all alone, staring at a room full of couples.

"I'm sorry you can't deal with this without trying to destroy yourself," she repeated under her breath. Perfect. Just the right touch of condescension.

Now to let him enjoy life without her for a while. See how much he liked it when he got what he *thought* he wanted. And then, she would simply wait until the right opportunity presented itself.

Claire smiled. It was unfair, it was dishonest, and it was certainly manipulative. But more important, with a little luck, it would probably work out just fine.

Zoey Passmore

I found the quiz in <u>Seventeen</u> or <u>Sassy</u> or <u>YM</u>, one of those, and tore it out. "How Well Do You Know Him?" with the word <u>Him</u> in bright pink letters. You're supposed to fill it out on your own first, guessing what your boyfriend's answer will be. Then later you ask your boyfriend, and if his answer is what you guessed it would be, great. If not, then you don't know him as well as you thought, right? Not that I take quizzes all that seriously. Still, I figured there had to be some validity to it or they wouldn't print

it in a serious magazine
like . . . like whichever one
it was in.

Anyway. The first ques-
tion was,

1 On the issue of sex, your boyfriend will
say he is willing to: (A) Put it off until
you are married; (B) Wait until you feel
the time is right and not pressure you till
then; (C) Pressure you to do it because once
you try it you'll like it; (D) Leave you and go
out with someone else if you keep saying no;
(E) Not applicable, we're already having sex.

Well. Kind of cuts right
to the heart of things,
doesn't it? First of all, we
can eliminate E right away.
I am not sleeping with
Lucas. I've never done it
with anyone. Not that I
haven't thought about it.
A lot. Especially when he's
kissing me and his hands
are . . . See? I'm thinking
about it right now.

But no. I don't know why, but that's like a step I'm not ready for yet. I think Lucas respects that. He doesn't respect it a lot; I mean, he's not thrilled by my saying no. Sometimes he's <u>very</u> not thrilled. But he wouldn't answer D. He also wouldn't answer A. I'm thinking he'll come down somewhere between a B and a C. Call it a C-plus. Although what he'll actually answer on the quiz is B, because he'll think that's the answer I want him to give.

LUCAS CABRAL

Forget E, unfortunately. If the answer were E, I

wouldn't be taking really
cold showers every night
after I say good night to
Zoey. If the answer were
E, I wouldn't be bouncing
off the walls and waking up
remembering dreams that,
believe me, you don't want
to hear about. Nope. Not E.

Not A, either. D is a
possibility; I mean, if this
goes on forever. Seriously,
say we're talking ten
years, we're both in our
late twenties? It's like
well into the twenty-
first century and I'm
still not getting laid? I
don't think so.

The true answer is C. Of
course. But I have to answer
B. I'm not an idiot.

Nina Geiger

Let's just set question one aside for a moment. Benjamin and I aren't even in the same room as that question. At least I'm not. I guess I don't know about him, given that we've only really had one date, which happened to be the first real date I ever had with anyone. I'm not exactly the Source of True Wisdom on this subject.

2 Your boyfriend's idea of a perfect date would be: (A) Going out for burgers and a movie; (B) Having a picnic on the beach and watching the sun go down; (C) Attending a rock concert; or (D) Hanging out with a big group of your mutual friends.

Easy. He'd like the concert, of course, over a movie. Benjamin's blind and he's big on music. But the answer he'd give if you asked him is B. Get it? Blind guy watching the sun go down? That's Benjamin's idea of funny. Mine too, actually.

BENJAMIN PASSMORE

B.

Aisha Gray

Question one, C Christopher isn't shy about asking. But then, I'm not shy about saying no Question two, I'd guess B because B would give him the best chance of getting back to question one.

Ah, question three. How appro-
priate

3 Will your boyfriend say that (A) You
are both free to see other people; (B)
He can see other girls but he expects
you to be faithful; (C) He'll be faithful to you
but he understands if you want to go out
with other guys; (D) Let's just see how it all
works out.

There it is, the question I
never asked but should have.
But would Christopher have
given me an honest answer?

That's the problem with quizzes.
They all depend on how honest
he is, how honest you are, and
how prepared you are to see the
truth. I'm guessing he'll
answer A. But I'm guessing
what he really means is B.

Christopher Shupe

I'VE BEEN LIVING IN AISHA'S
HOUSE WHILE I RECUPERATED FROM A
VERY UNFORTUNATE RUN-IN WITH
SOME GUYS WHO DIDN'T APPRECIATE
THE COLOR OF MY SKIN. I'M HAVING
MEALS COOKED FOR ME BY AISHA'S
MOTHER, AND BOOKS BROUGHT TO ME
BY AISHA'S FATHER. AISHA'S
LITTLE BROTHER COMES AROUND AND
PLAYS VIDEO GAMES WITH ME. I
WOULD HAVE TO BE A BIGGER TOAD
THAN I AM TO ANSWER A UNDER
THESE CIRCUMSTANCES, KNOWING HOW
AISHA FEELS. I GUESS IF YOU
REALLY TWISTED MY ARM, I'D SAY
MY HEARTFELT ANSWER WOULD BE B.
BUT I DON'T KNOW ANYMORE. AISHA
HAS STUCK BY ME BIG TIME. THAT
COUNTS FOR A LOT. I ALSO HAPPEN

TO LIKE HER MORE THAN ANY GIRL
I'VE EVER MET.

MY ANSWER IS D. I GUESS. ASK
ME AGAIN LATER WHEN I'M TOTALLY
BACK ON MY FEET.

One

The waves were more gray than blue, and when Lucas stood up on his board, his longish blond hair was the only splash of color in a tableau of sea and sky that could almost have been a black-and-white photograph.

Zoey Passmore pulled the cowl neck of her sweater up over her chin and ears and slid her hands up inside the sleeves. The beach sand had lost all of the warmth from the sun that had shone so encouragingly earlier in the day, and she kept to the blanket. She'd collected driftwood from the beach and fallen limbs from the pine trees behind her and piled them with ex-Girl Scout expertise in a nice little pyramid. But she didn't want to light the fire until Lucas was with her for fear she'd burn up all her stash of fuel before he finally got tired of surfing.

Lucas fell from the board, diving into the water headfirst and surfacing moments later to shake the water from his hair like a dog. He grinned and held up a single finger, indicating one more wave.

She watched him reclaim his board and paddle back out, black rubber tight on his legs and butt, his feet bare and probably frozen by now. But she couldn't begrudge him the opportunity. There were rarely surfable waves on Chatham Island. This was a fluke, the result of a major storm far out over the Atlantic. It had brought them just the skirts of its clouds and enough of a surge to send Lucas scrambling to wax his old board and squeeze himself into a wet suit he'd clearly outgrown.

He caught a wave and had a good, long ride, bringing the board within a few feet of the narrow beach before he tumbled.

But he kept his word and emerged from the surf, lifting his board free of the foam that surged to within a couple of yards of Zoey's feet.

"Quick, light the fire!" he yelled. "I'm numb."

Zoey smiled. His hair was wet and tousled, his body outlined in perfect detail by the tight wet suit. She felt a definite twinge. He looked incredible. Too incredible for Zoey's own good. She fished in her bag for the matches, but without taking her eyes from him.

She tore her eyes away and found the matches. He planted his surfboard upright in the sand and flopped onto the blanket beside her, smelling of salt and laughing in sheer delight.

"Damn, I'd forgotten how much I loved that." He pulled the zipper halfway down his chest and inhaled deeply. "If only I'd been able to breathe. I guess I'll have to break down and buy a new suit."

Zoey struck a match, but it was instantly blown out by the wind. *Don't say it,* she warned herself. *Don't say it.*

Then she said it anyway. "I think that suit looks pretty good on you." Her voice wobbled a little and she concentrated on lighting a second match, cupping it in her hands. She touched the flame to the dried grass kindling. It crackled loudly and caught fire.

Lucas rolled toward her and without warning stuck his hands under her sweater, pressing them to her bare stomach.

Zoey squealed and tried to push him away, but he held on. "Get those icicles off me!"

"I can't wait for the fire," he said. "I need warmth now. My hands are numb."

"I warned you it was freezing out there. You're the one who said 'Don't worry, I'll be plenty warm in my wet suit.'"

Lucas slid his hands around her back and drew her against him. Then he rolled onto his back, still holding her tight. "My lips are numb, too."

Zoey lowered her mouth to his and kissed his cold lips. She closed her eyes and kissed him again, more deeply, a vision of him rising from the surf still firmly fixed in her mind. Within seconds his lips were as warm as her own. She kissed his cheeks and pressed her hands to them. She kissed his eyelids and his neck.

"Now are you warm?" Zoey asked.

14

"Mmm. Now even other parts of me are warm," he said.

"Don't be crude."

"I meant my feet."

"Sure you did," Zoey said. She gave him a light peck on the lips and rolled off him. "Are you hungry?"

"That depends. Is there anything *else* on the menu? I mean besides food. You know, maybe something for some *other* form of hunger?"

"We have hot dogs and we have s'mores. That's what's on the menu."

Lucas sighed. "Okay, then I guess I'm hungry." There was no mistaking the pouting tone in his voice.

"Lucas, I thought we were going to give that topic a rest," Zoey said testily.

Lucas sat up and wrapped his arms around his knees. "I'm sorry. But you know, one thing kind of leads to another. We make out, we touch each other, first thing you know, I'm thinking about the next step. It's like . . . like saying hey, we'll get all dressed up, we'll drive to a fancy restaurant, we'll sit down and order this great meal, only, surprise, we're not going to eat anything."

Zoey was silent for a moment while the fire snapped and spread a glow around them. "You're using a food example. You must be hungry."

"I'm starving," he admitted ruefully.

"Look, Lucas, if every time we make out you're going to say I'm leading you toward sex,

15

then what am I supposed to do?" She held up her hand quickly. "Scratch that question. My point is, I really, really like kissing you. Really, really. But I'm not going to be able to enjoy it if you keep saying step one has to lead to step two has to lead to step three when I'm not ready for step three. You know?"

Lucas shrugged and looked away. Then he looked back at her, dissatisfied but not angry. "So if I want one and two, I have to shut up about three."

Zoey sighed heavily. It wasn't like she never considered step three. They weren't all that different, not really, she and Lucas. Except that it was more complicated for her than for him. It must be nice to be a guy and have everything be so simple and straightforward—just be led around by your hormones and never have to think about consequences. "Lucas, don't you want this to be a choice I can make for myself, one way or the other, and that I can feel good about?"

He absorbed that for a moment and winced. "Yeah, yeah," he said, making no attempt at sincerity.

Zoey smiled and hugged him. "We can still do some more of steps one and two."

"Okay. But first, we eat."

Zoey said good-bye to Lucas as night fell over Chatham Island and the tiny village of North Harbor. He went off toward his home, tired from the surf and, Zoey was sure, still a bit disgruntled and unsatisfied. She herself was feeling edgy, as she often did after making out with Lucas. She'd intended to go straight home and finish the journalism class assignment that was hanging over her head, but she didn't feel like concentrating. She was full of pent-up energy. She waved her arms back and forth at her sides, realizing how strange it would look to anyone who might be out on the streets and saw her.

She decided to stop by Nina's house. Zoey hadn't talked to her since the night before at the homecoming dance. Normally Nina could be counted on to drop by on just about any day of the week, especially a weekend day. But so far the day had been Nina-less.

Zoey walked the length of Center Street, crossing to walk through the parklike center of the circle. An island car, muffler blasting, front bumper held on by string, came rattling by and Zoey waved. Mrs. Gray, Aisha's mother. There were few of the island's three hundred permanent residents Zoey didn't recognize.

She reached Lighthouse Road, the northern edge of the island where cobblestones, low picket fences, and neatly tended gardens ran into sharp-edged, slick-wet rocks and sudden explosions of ocean spray. She went in through the gate of the Geiger house and instinctively looked up at the widow's walk, a railed deck atop the third story of the old house. Sure

17

enough, there was Claire Geiger, Nina's sister. She was wearing a bright yellow rain slicker. Her long, voluptuous black hair streamed out from under an incongruous yellow rain hat.

"Damn," Zoey said under her breath. She herself was still wearing just a sweater, no coat.

Claire peered down, leaning casually on the rickety-looking railing. "Hey, Zoey."

"Hi, Claire. It's going to rain, huh?" Zoey yelled up at her, craning her neck.

"Zoey, we are completely blanketed with nimbostratus."

"Uh-huh," Zoey said.

"Rain clouds. Nimbostratus. But forget these." She waved a hand dismissively. "This is nothing. What's great is that there's a monster Canadian cold front rolling down toward upstate New York and Vermont."

"Yeah, that's cool, all right," Zoey said dryly. If Claire hadn't had the good luck to be very beautiful and endowed with a natural elegance that emerged even from beneath a rain slicker, she would have spent her life as a nerd. Yet because she was the person she was, her fascination with weather, her natural solitude, her distant reserve all added to a sense that she was a unique individual, not to be judged by anyone's standards but her own. Whatever *those* might be.

"Snow," Claire said, her eyes glowing as if she were announcing the advent of universal world peace. "There's a serious possibility of major

18

snow in Vermont. Say, around . . . Killington? And next weekend is a three-day weekend?"

Zoey clicked. "Ski trip? Are you thinking ski trip?"

Claire smiled her infrequent smile. "Very likely. I'll let you know."

"Excellent," Zoey said enthusiastically. She and Claire didn't share much (except for some ex-boyfriends), but they did both like to ski. And even though the school year was less than two months old, Zoey had been feeling hemmed in lately. A road trip would be just the thing.

She had no idea whether Lucas would like the idea. He'd never mentioned skiing. But snowboarding was very similar to surfing.

And yet, it brought up the question of spending a weekend with Lucas away from family.

"Where would we stay?" Zoey yelled up.

"My dad knows a guy with a condo there. This early in the year he won't have rented it," Claire said. She smiled knowingly. "Don't worry, I'm sure there will be plenty of beds for whatever arrangement you want."

Zoey knocked at the front door and went on in. She followed the sound of the Red Hot Chili Peppers up the stairs to Nina's room. She banged on Nina's door.

"Qué día tan hermoso!"

She went inside and found Nina Geiger

19

lying on her back on the bed, feet up on the wall, holding a Spanish textbook above her head. She was shouting phrases over the music, singsong Spanish intermingling with the cheerfully defiant obscenity coming from the stereo.

"Cree usted que hara buen tiempo mañana?"

"Nina!" Zoey yelled at the top of her lungs.

Nina looked alarmed, then smiled. "Zoey. *Chiquita. Como está?"*

Zoey sat on the bed and stretched to turn down the music. She and Nina did not share musical tastes. In fact, on a surface level they shared almost nothing. Nina was a year younger, louder, funnier, stranger, more vulnerable despite everything, and tended to dress like a refugee from Seattle by way of a rest stop in New York. The two of them had been best friends for years.

"I just stopped by to say hi," Zoey said. "You didn't come over today."

Nina shrugged and looked away evasively. "I am so behind on homework, Zoey. In history class I'm behind by an entire war. And in Modern Media I'm just media-ocre."

Zoey made a disgusted face at her pun. "Don't tell me you're hiding out because you have homework. Do I look dumb enough to believe that?"

"I thought it was worth a try."

"Come on, Nina. You didn't come over because you didn't want to run into Benjamin."

Nina rolled over and searched for her purse.

"That's not it," she said. "That would be silly and immature, and as we both know, I am the model of maturity."

"Things didn't go too well between you guys?" Zoey asked reluctantly. She had promised herself she would not, under any circumstances, get involved in the tentative relationship between her best friend and her brother. But this wasn't getting involved, exactly. She was just making conversation.

"Things went fine," Nina said. She continued to avoid Zoey's gaze, searching through her purse. She found a pack of Lucky Strikes and stuck one in her mouth, as always leaving it unlit.

"Look, you can tell me. Nothing you say will embarrass me."

"Okay, Zoey, since you asked. After the dance Benjamin and I stripped naked and made love like animals in the mud in the middle of the football field."

For a split second, Zoey's heart stopped. Then she sighed. "Okay, there *are* some things you could say that might embarrass me," she admitted.

Nina looked pleased with herself, as she always did when she managed to get a reaction out of someone. "Actually, it was no big deal."

"It was your first date, Nina."

"Didn't Benjamin already tell you what happened?"

"I don't talk to my brother about his love

life," Zoey said. "I talk to my best friend about my brother's love life. Now, I promise I will never get involved again, in any way, or even ask so much as a single question, but come on, Nina. I mean, this was a big thing for you."

After years of silence Nina had recently accused her uncle of molesting her as a child. One of Nina's deepest scars from that experience was a lingering fear of the opposite sex. Zoey knew that what would have been just a date for most girls was an act of courage for Nina.

"Well, we danced."

"I know. I saw that part," Zoey said patiently. "I was there."

"We held hands. It was sort of like you told me it would be. Only my hands kept getting sweaty, and I never knew when we were supposed to stop, or after we stopped when we should start again."

"That's good, though," Zoey said, feeling a wave of affection for her friend. "You got through it, right?"

Nina nodded. "Yeah. But it was close. I mean, when we kissed—"

"You what?"

"We went outside and, you know . . ."

"Is this another joke?"

"No. I kissed him, all right? Jeez. I guess I should have taken pictures."

"Where did you kiss him?"

"Outside?"

"You know what I mean," Zoey said.

22

"On the mouth. Actually, I missed on the first try and kissed his nose. But the second one was full lip contact. No tongue, though," she added helpfully.

This detail was just half a step too far for Zoey. "Okay, there is something sick about this. I mean, if it were any other guy, I'd be asking for all the gory details. But it's *Benjamin*."

"Yeah." Nina smiled wistfully. She nodded. "It was nice. I mean, a couple of times all the old stuff with my uncle started coming back, and I was getting panicky. A couple of times I was close to blowing punch and Doritos all over Benjamin."

"That would have been romantic," Zoey said, grinning at the image.

"But then I said, no, this is Benjamin, not someone else, and it's right now, not back then. And so then I was mostly liking it."

"Mostly?"

"Like papayas." Nina sucked thoughtfully on the cigarette.

"Papayas."

"You know, like it's unfamiliar, you haven't tasted it before, so you're cautious. It's not something you're sure of, like watermelon or apples. Then you start thinking, well, it's new and different, but it's not bad. I could see where over time I could develop a taste for this."

"That's good."

"Yeah." She looked up at the ceiling. "Yeah. Only . . . I don't know what Benjamin thought. I mean, he's tasted papayas before. He's tasted them with Claire, in fact. And she's a much more experienced papaya than I am."

"Oh, I get it. So you're worried about what Benjamin thought. Like did he enjoy it as much as you did."

"Or maybe it was just a pity date all along. And maybe he thought *no way*." She bit her lip.

"You shouldn't worry about him and Claire. I think that's over. It's Jake she's interested in now."

"Oh, *really*?" Nina said. "So how come she broke up with Jake at the dance?"

Zoey's mouth dropped open. "She dumped him? Poor Jake."

"Yeah, yeah, poor Jake. That's not what's important. Benjamin and Claire were *a thing* for a long time, as in years. Benjamin and I have been *a thing* for, let's see, almost twenty-four hours."

"I don't think Claire would go after your boyfriend, Nina," Zoey said, trying to sound convincing.

"Please. Claire would snatch a cookie out of the hand of a starving orphan. I'm not saying she would enjoy it, but if she felt she had to . . . I've tried to tell you," Nina went on, wagging her finger, "she worships Satan up there on that widow's walk. In fact, Claire gets Satan to do her homework for her. Last week he slept over and they made popcorn and stayed up all night watching reruns on

Nick at Night. Satan is especially fond of *F Troop*, it turns out."

"Are you done?"

"Yeah, I think so."

"Look. If you're worried about how Benjamin feels, you could just ask him," Zoey suggested.

Nina looked half-troubled and half-sly. "Or maybe someone else could find out for me." She batted her eyes.

"Oh no. I am not getting in the middle of you and Benjamin. No way."

Nina shrugged and fell serious. "I guess we'll work it out. I mean, Benjamin and I are good friends no matter what, right? One date, one kiss won't suddenly change everything. Will it?"

Probably, Zoey thought. "Everything will be fine," she said out loud.

Two

Christopher Shupe was living in greater luxury than he had ever seen outside of a movie or *Lifestyles of the Rich and Famous*. The bedroom was twice the size of any normal bedroom. It would have been possible to fit the entire two-bedroom project apartment where he'd grown up into this one room. The high, plush four-poster bed, as big as it was, with flowery draped fabric, voluminous matching down comforter, and some form of pillow covers that Aisha's mother insisted on calling shams, looked tiny in the overall space.

The floor was polished dark wood, partly covered with thick rugs. The walls were papered, trimmed in little flowery decals. The curtains were heavy and multilayered. He had a couch and a love seat and a coffee table. He had a tall oak dresser and a curved, oak-framed mirror.

And that was just the bedroom. He also got a separate dressing room, whatever that was about. And a monstrous closet that made his few articles of clothing look paltry.

But it was the bathroom that was truly amazing. There were endless miles of tiled countertops and a stalled shower, but by far the coolest feature was the raised whirlpool bath. He could lie in the whirlpool up to his chest in hot, foaming currents, and look out the window, down over the lights of North Harbor.

At the moment he was doing just that, though his attention was drawn to the small color TV showing a late-running football game. The remote control was on the tile beside him, alongside a cold soda.

It was a fine life, although very temporary. Too bad it had come as a consequence of getting beaten up. He still had to keep his bandaged arm and stitched face out of the water, but the heat felt wonderful on the bruises covering his legs and stomach and back.

Christopher heard a distant knock on the bedroom door and Aisha's voice.

"Come in!" he yelled.

The door opened. "Are you in the bathroom?"

"Yeah. But I'm jacuzzing. Don't worry. I won't show you anything you don't want to see."

Aisha Gray appeared, framed by the bathroom door, tall, thin, graceful, topped by a volcano of bouncy dark curls. "Stay in the water," she warned. "My mom wants to know if you think you can make it downstairs for dinner. If not, she'll bring you something up here."

"I can more or less walk up and down stairs," Christopher said. "But I don't know if your mom and dad and Kalif want to stare at my face through dinner." He indicated the stitches and the blood redness in one eye.

"You don't look so bad," Aisha said. Sweetly, it seemed to Christopher. She sat down at the far edge of the raised tile platform. "Besides, Kalif would love it. He thinks stitches are tough. He wants some of his own."

"Let's hope not, huh?" Christopher felt the cloud forming over him again. Suppressed rage and frustration that could only be kept under control by concentrating on the revenge he had promised himself. He forced a smile. "With all this luxury, you guys are going to have a hard time getting rid of me."

"I told my mom to put you in one of the cheap rooms," Aisha said. "But this room is her pride and joy. You know, in summer this rents out for two hundred and fifty dollars a day, not counting tax. Of course, a continental breakfast is included."

"Your mom is very cool," Christopher said with feeling. As soon as she'd learned of the beating Christopher had taken, Mrs. Gray had offered the facilities of the bed-and-breakfast as a place for him to recover. He had no family in the area, and no family capable of helping any-where.

"She has that nurturing thing going big time," Aisha said fondly. "But I told her not to be stuffing pastries down you, making you fat."

Christopher nodded. "How about you,

Aisha? No nurturing instincts?"

"Why? You need additional nurturing?"

"I *need* you to come over here and kiss me."

Aisha gave him a dubious look. "You're taking a bath."

"So close your eyes."

Aisha slid closer but stayed just out of reach. "I don't know, Christopher. It's not like we've settled everything between us. We were broken up before this whole thing happened. And I seem to remember that it was your fault."

She wasn't exactly saying no. More like she was looking for some reassurance. "Aisha, do you really believe that I'm thinking about any girl but you right now?"

"Maybe not *right now*," Aisha said. "But five minutes from now?"

"Are you going to kiss me or not?"

Aisha looked him over thoughtfully. She had an uncanny way of slipping into an observational mode that reminded him of a scientist watching bacteria through a microscope. It was part of what made her so interesting—she was always precariously balanced between cool, skeptical reason and blind, impetuous romance.

Aisha bit her lip and shook her head ruefully, and Christopher knew that romance had gained the upper hand. For the moment, at least. She moved closer and put her hand to his bruised cheek. Her fingers were cool. She lowered her face toward his, closing her black eyes slowly. Her lips met his.

He returned the kiss, feeling it spread throughout his body like a painkiller. Her lips were so soft. Her touch so gentle. Her hair fell around his face, almost closing off the outside world.

Why couldn't he just tell her that he would be faithful? And mean it? She had been at his side the instant she knew he was hurt. She was at his side now. She was beautiful and passionate and he had never, with any other girl, felt the way he did at this moment with Aisha.

He opened his eyes and saw that hers were still closed. Through her curls he caught a glimpse of the TV, and of the L.A. Rams cheerleaders.

Still, he reminded himself, there were so many girls in the world. Why should he accept limits? Even the delicious limits imposed by Aisha's full, soft lips?

Aisha pulled away, but only an inch. "I do love you," she whispered. "I wish I didn't, but I do."

What should he say? Did he love her back? Yes, he did love her. Yes, of that he was certain. It *was* love. But should he say it? Would she think it was some sort of vow?

The hesitation was fatal. She drew back, pushing her hair out of her face.

"Aisha . . ." he began.

She stood up, keeping her eyes averted. "Dinner is in about fifteen minutes," she said. "I'll have my mom bring it up to you."

*   *   *

Claire climbed down the ladder that led from the widow's walk back to her room, feeling wet and elated. The storm hadn't been much more than a lazy drizzle. A disappointment, as she'd been hoping for some good lightning. But Zoey had jumped at the idea of a road trip to Vermont. And Zoey would convince Nina to come along, and what Zoey and Nina did, Aisha could be convinced to go along with. That would mean all four girls, plus of course Lucas, who would certainly come with Zoey; Christopher, if he was well enough and getting along with Aisha by then; even Benjamin, if Nina hadn't found some way to alienate him on their one date. Benjamin and Nina. Claire shook her head. She might get used to that concept eventually, but it would take time.

Anyway, if the entire contingent of island kids went away for the weekend, wouldn't Jake want to go, too? Jake was the most fanatic skier of the group. Of course he'd go—as long as it looked like a nonromantic, noncouple, group sort of thing.

Claire shucked off her raincoat and hat and hung them on the closet hook. She spread a towel under them to soak up the dripping rainwater.

She would have to make clear to Jake that she considered it over between them. It wouldn't be about the two of them being together. It would just be about enjoying some

31

early snow and being off the island. A group thing. And the trick would be getting someone else to invite him.

Then if, while they were off at some romantic mountain hideaway, things very innocently developed between Jake and Claire . . . Well, it would be Jake's own choice, wouldn't it?

Claire quickly changed her blouse and started downstairs toward the aroma of clam chowder and Janelle's homemade corn muffins.

She ran into Nina and Zoey on the second-floor landing.

"What are you grinning about?" Nina demanded, looking suspicious. "You look like you're up to something."

"Are you going to stay for dinner, Zoey?" Claire asked, ignoring her sister and wiping the telltale smile off her face.

"No, I'm heading home. But thanks."

The three of them descended the stairs. "Have you told Nina about the snow?" Claire asked.

"No. We were talking about . . . other stuff," Zoey said cryptically.

Benjamin, Claire realized with a surprising pang. *Stupid,* she told herself sternly. It was absurd to be planning to win back Jake while at the same time feeling a sense of loss every time Benjamin's name came up. Chatham Island was getting too small. Too many former boyfriends lying around.

"What about snow?" Nina asked.

"We're thinking road trip this weekend," Claire said. "There's supposed to be a snowstorm moving through Vermont, and with that, plus the man-made snow, Zoey and I were thinking maybe we'd head to Killington. Me, Zoey, and I assume, Lucas."

"Well, Nina, you'd come, too, wouldn't you?" Zoey said quickly.

Claire fought the urge to smile. The mental image of just the three of them—Zoey, Lucas, and Claire—hadn't set too well with Zoey. She wanted Nina along, too. But Nina was looking dubious. "Oh, Nina doesn't want to come," Claire said.

"You don't want me along, Claire? I'm hurt," Nina said.

They paused in the entryway. "It's not that I don't want you along, Nina—" Claire let the sentence hang. Of course she *did* want her sister along, if Nina could bring Benjamin and add to the sense it was just one big happy island family. But Nina would do the opposite of whatever Claire wanted.

"If you guys are going, *I'm* going," Nina announced.

"You don't even ski," Claire pointed out.

"Maybe I'll learn. I'm a work in progress, Claire. I intend to do lots of things in my life that I haven't done before. Be a roadie for Pearl Jam. Get a tattoo on my left butt cheek. Shave all your hair off while you're asleep some night.

It's a busy life, but I could probably find the time to learn to ski."

"You might even enjoy it," Zoey suggested helpfully.

"Don't push it, Zo," Nina said. "No offense, but only an idiot could enjoy hurtling uncontrollably down a slope while their ears freeze and break off."

"So, you're in," Claire said, trying to sound annoyed. Easy enough, really, since Nina had a natural talent for annoying her.

"Yeah."

Claire sighed and headed toward the dining room. Now, with her back turned, she could allow herself an impish smile. Easy. So easy.

"Well, then I guess one of you two should invite Benjamin," Claire called over her shoulder.

34

4 Which of the following ten descriptions would your boyfriend agree apply to you?

Claire Geiger

Well, what an interesting question. It would be even more interesting if I were sure who my boyfriend was. In my mind it's still Jake, though technically I broke up with him at the homecoming dance. But it isn't that simple. I, mean, I broke it off because that's what he needed me to do. He couldn't reconcile being in love with me and blaming me for the death of his brother, Wade, two years ago. It was tearing him up, and me pressuring him to get over it wasn't helping.

So I told him it was over. I think the military phrase for it is **tactical** **retreat**.

Which of the following ten descriptions would my boyfriend agree apply to me? I'll give it a shot, though I'm not sure when or if I'll ever be able to get Jake's answers.

1. Manipulative. Yes, Jake would have to go along with that. And what can I do? Deny it? That would seem even more manipulative.

2. Vain. No.

3. Beautiful. Yes. And no, that does not prove I'm vain.

I know I'm attractive, but I honestly don't care that much. Although it can be useful.

3. Giving. That might be stretching the facts a little.

4. Friendly. That would also be stretching the facts a little.

5. Romantic. More than people think, but I doubt Jake would answer yes to it. I genuinely am in love with Jake. Sure, I'm willing to be a little manipulative in pursuit of some happiness, but that doesn't make the emotion any less sincere. So, yes, I am a romantic.

Just not one who thinks romance is all about heavy sighs and soulful looks. Jake would answer no.

6. Intelligent. Yes. And Jake would say yes as well. In fact, I think he s a little intimidated.

7. Sensual. Less than most people think. I have the sense that people have an incorrect opinion of me here. Probably. I wouldn't really know because I don't spend a lot of time trying to guess what people are thinking about me. It would be interesting to see Jake's answer to this one, though. I imagine, like most guys, he would hope the answer is yes.

8. Funny. I don't know. I'm not Nina, obviously. And I don't remember Jake and me ever laughing much. We had a relationship that had about one good week before it entered this sort of continuing crisis. The Cold

War, Part Two. Right now he'd answer no to this, just to annoy me.

9. Loyal. Another tough one. I don't think any of the guys I've gone out with would say yes to this. Which I guess is too bad. I suppose the truth is that my main loyalty is to myself, and despite everything I've tried to do to show my loyalty to Jake, I doubt he would give me a point here. Someday, maybe. Not yet.

10. Good. Oh, there's a deceptively sneaky one from the old quizmaster. Am I a good person? Benjamin once told me that deep down inside I was fundamentally decent, and could be counted on to do

the right thing. And Benjamin is a
perceptive person. But he's also still
in love with me, so perhaps his
judgment is wrong. I don't think Jake
thinks of me as a good person, though
I know he's still in love with me as
well. All I can say is that I always
try to do what's right. As long as
the right thing is also the thing that
works.

Three

"What am I supposed to do? Do I sit with you?
Do I sit with him? Do I say hi to him, then
come sit with you? Do I ignore him unless he
says hi to me, or unless he sits with me? I don't
understand any of this. Isn't there a book somewhere that explains it all? *The Big Book o'
Relationships?*"

Nina found the pack of Lucky Strikes in her
purse and stuck one, unlit, in the corner of her
mouth. The chill sea breeze fretted her dark
hair, stinging her cheeks and eyes. She drew her
jacket around her, comforted by the warmth and
the satisfying groan of the leather. She glared
across the deck of the ferry at Benjamin, who
was listening to music through earphones and
hiding his blank eyes behind black Ray•Bans.

"I am absolutely *not* going to get involved in
your relationship with my brother," Zoey announced firmly. "I meant what I said yesterday.
That was it. Never again." She was sitting beside Nina on the bench, shivering because, as
usual, she had not dressed warmly enough.
She'd spent nearly her entire life in Maine but

still clung to what Nina thought was an inappropriate optimism about the weather. Now Zoey was holding her wispy blond hair down with her hands, trying to keep her ears warm. "What you do with Benjamin is your problem, and his. I'm not advising, I'm not passing information back and forth, I'm not spying for either of you."

Nina gave her a dirty look. "Zoey, why do you have bare legs when it's this cold? You're a senior; figure it out. It's cold. And it's distracting, having to talk to someone who is turning blue and rattling. Especially someone who doesn't understand that girl-girl solidarity transcends mere sister-brother solidarity."

"*You* have bare legs," Zoey said. "I mean, those tights aren't exactly warm."

"Yes, but I have hot legs. I always have. My upper body gets cold, but my legs are unnaturally hot. At night sometimes I have to stick them out from under the blankets."

"I never knew that about you," Zoey said dryly.

"Oh, yeah. Hot-leg Nina—new from Mattel. I'll be Barbie's newest, coolest friend."

Zoey laughed. "See, this is why I can't give you advice. I have my own selfish interests. I mean, if you start sitting with Benjamin every day, who'll sit with me and keep me from doing my homework on the way in to school?"

"I notice Lucas doesn't always sit with us," Nina pointed out. "So I figured maybe there

42

was some *thing* I didn't know about. Some secret agreement everyone but me knows about that says boyfriends and girlfriends don't sit together at certain times. A state law or something. Like at lunch it's always just you and me and Aisha. And Claire, whenever she feels like hanging with her inferiors."

Zoey shrugged. "These things just work out. I mean, I spend lots of time with Lucas. He's over every night. Wait, backspace—every *evening*. He's over every evening."

"Hey, Eesh," Nina said, reaching around Zoey's back to poke Aisha.

Aisha looked up from her notebook, where she'd been busily scribbling calculus problems. "What?"

"I just wanted to see if you were conscious," Nina said.

"I'm trying to get my calc done so I don't have to do it during lunch."

"Hmm," Nina said, nudging Zoey. "Aisha is behind on her homework. That's fact number one. And fact number two is that Christopher is now living with her. Do I sense a connection there somewhere?"

Aisha slapped her pen against her pad. "He is not living with me. I happen to live in a B&B. Strangers often stay there. It's the whole point of a B&B. Christopher is no more living with me than any of the old fart couples who come and spend a weekend."

"Touchy, isn't she?" Nina said gleefully.

"How is Christopher doing?" Zoey asked.

"He's recovering pretty well. Mostly he's living it up while my mom stuffs the latest recipe from *Gourmet* magazine down his throat."

"Do you think he'll want to go skiing?" Nina asked.

"Do I think he'll want to go skiing?" Aisha repeated. "Yes, Nina. That was the very first thing he asked for this morning when he woke up. He said, 'Hey, I'd like to go skiing.'"

"Ha," Nina pounced. "So you were there with him *when he woke up.*"

"It was a figure of speech." Aisha closed her notebook with an air of resignation. "Christopher is unfortunately still a partial toad. He's an injured toad I am helping take care of out of the goodness of my heart, but he's still a toad."

"Huh. So, you guys don't want to go skiing?" Nina asked.

"What is this with skiing?" Aisha exploded.

"Claire says it's going to snow in Vermont," Zoey said.

Aisha threw up her hands. "It's like having a conversation with Beavis and Butt-head. Would one of you explain to me what you are talking about?"

Nina raised her hand. "Can I be Butt-head? Zoey's the blond."

"We're thinking about taking a road trip over to Vermont this weekend," Zoey explained. "It's supposed to snow, and Claire says she can get us all a condo at Killington. Claire and I both like to ski."

"It's an excellent way to make yourself into a paraplegic," Nina said.

Aisha shrugged. "I don't think Christopher would be up for skiing by then. Besides, I really doubt he skis."

"Lucas doesn't either, but I figured since he likes to surf, he'd probably get into snowboarding."

"I don't do either," Nina said. "I just drink hot chocolate and sing 'Walkin' in a Winter Wonderland' over and over until people threaten to kill me."

"Sounds like fun," Aisha said dubiously.

"First it has to snow," Zoey said. "Then we have to get all the parental units to go along."

"Are you asking Benjamin?" Aisha asked Nina.

"Sure," Nina said with more confidence than she felt. "I'll ask him later. Unless Zoey would just be a good friend and ask him for me."

"This looks like a boyfriend-girlfriend situation, *not* a brother-sister situation," Zoey said.

"Except for Claire, who is currently boy-friendless," Aisha noted.

Nina nodded thoughtfully. "Yeah. Unless for some reason Jake decides to come along." She glanced across the deck at Claire, who was sitting alone, reading a book. A shadow of suspicion crossed Nina's mind. This whole trip was Claire's idea.

But no, not even Claire was that subtle.

* * *

45

Benjamin ran his finger along the curved brass railing as he descended the stairs from the top deck to the bottom deck. One, two, three . . . fifteen stairs, counted off almost without thinking. He turned a sharp right, advanced to the next railing, and, so naturally that a casual observer would not have known he was blind, he trailed a finger along the painted brass to the gangway.

Once on the dock he needed a landmark to locate himself. The ferry landing was imprecise, and he needed precision. He unfolded his cane, swung it in a short arc and quickly found the bench he was seeking. Now, in a line with the bench, it would be fifty-two paces to the curb at the end of the dock.

He heard a person fall into step with him and guessed from a host of almost imperceptible clues that it was Nina.

"Hi, Nina," he said with a smile. "You can't fool me just because you change brands of soap."

"Damn," Nina said. "I went from Dove to Irish Spring. It's manly, yes, but I like it, too."

"Yeah, but you stayed with Lucky Strikes. The smell of tobacco but no smoke. Dead giveaway. Plus Doc Martens make a certain sound. So do tights when your legs rub together." He put on a cocky swagger. "Don't mess with me, Nina. I have powers far beyond anything you puny earthlings could comprehend."

"Oh yeah? What color underwear do I have

on? And my legs do not rub together."

"White. All cotton."

There was a long silence. "Okay, I give up," Nina said.

Benjamin grinned. "Just a lucky guess."

"Okay. Try this. How many fingers am I holding up?"

"One. The middle one. That was too easy." He was rewarded by the sound of Nina's laughter, a sound that conveyed a sort of unforced, childlike delight. It was a sound that always touched a soft spot in Benjamin.

Laughs were telling, he had discovered. Claire's was rare and dryly appreciative. Bestowed like a pat on the back for a job well done. Zoey always sounded surprised, as if she hadn't been expecting to laugh but wow! now she was and she was glad about it. Aisha had two—a restrained, moderate one that was partly just politeness, and a wilder one that broke out like an escaped animal she couldn't quite get under control.

"So, look, Benjamin," Nina began in the awkward way she had of shifting into a serious topic. "I was wondering. I mean, usually on Monday after school I come over and read to you."

"Yes."

"Well, do you want me to come over and read to you today as usual?"

"Sure. Why not?"

"No reason. I was just asking."

They reached the curb and Benjamin turned

toward the crosswalk. In a corner of his mind the count went on, a subliminal reassurance that he knew where he was, could place himself in the invisible world. "I still want you to keep reading, unless you decide you don't want to."

"Do you *want* me to decide I don't want to?" Nina asked.

"No, I want you to decide that you *do* want to. Unless you really don't want to."

"I want to."

"Which? Keep reading? Or not?"

"Whichever you want," Nina said.

Benjamin groaned. "Nina, this isn't supposed to happen. Even though we went out together, we're supposed to go on being friends. Friends first. That was the deal."

"So . . . so you're saying the other thing, that was just the one time?"

"Is that what you want?" Benjamin asked.

"No fair. I asked you first. Come on, light's green."

They crossed the street. Benjamin could hear the idling car engines on his left and the electronic click as the light went to yellow. Some distance ahead he could hear Zoey's voice, raised in conversation with Lucas.

"I had a good time the other night," Benjamin said.

"Me too," Nina said guardedly. "The music was pretty bad, but it was fun anyway. I mean, dancing and all."

Was Nina trying to tell him something? Had

she been turned off by the kiss they had shared? It was certainly possible. She was just starting to deal with the corrosive aftermath of the situation with her uncle. Maybe she hadn't felt good about kissing Benjamin. Maybe she wasn't ready to go that far.

Or maybe she just didn't like *him* in that way. Maybe it wasn't some general thing, maybe it was specific. She'd avoided coming over on Sunday. And just now, on the ferry, she hadn't even come over to say hello.

"Yeah, dancing," Benjamin said, distracted by his own thoughts.

A silence descended that lasted several minutes. "So. I'll come over this afternoon and read for a couple of hours," Nina said.

Was she sounding relieved? No, that wasn't quite it. But she sounded strange. "That would be great," Benjamin said.

Four

"There is no doubt but that as we move into the electronic environment of the near future we will see changes in the craft of journalism," Mr. Schwarz said. "But the basics will still be much the same. It will still be a matter of conveying the facts, giving those facts context, and—"

The bell rang, ending first period. Instantly books were gathered up, feet shuffled, desks scraped on the floor.

"—I guess I'll leave you all in suspense until tomorrow," Mr. Schwarz said. "Zoey? Can you stay for a moment? The rest of you, take off. But don't forget I want your assignments on my desk by Thursday, no excuses."

Zoey hung back as the rest of the class rushed past. She picked up her books and papers and went up to the desk, wondering if she'd done something wrong or blown some test. But as she searched her memory, she couldn't imagine what it might be.

"What did you want, Mr. Schwarz?" He was, without a doubt, the best-looking teacher at Weymouth High: tall, fairly young for a teacher, with brown rock-star hair.

He wiggled his eyebrows suggestively. "I got a call from Lisa Soo at the *Weymouth Times*."

Lisa Soo was the assistant style editor at the city newspaper, which put her in charge of the twice-a-month youth section, written by students from all the high schools in the area. Zoey had done articles for her during her junior year.

"What did she do, find a misspelled word from one of my old stories?" Zoey asked, not wanting to seem too eager.

"No, she has an assignment for us, and I suggested you'd be the person for the job."

Zoey felt a thrill of anticipation. It was just the youth page, but it was for a real paper. Those kinds of clips, along with her contributions to the high school paper, would help get her on the student paper when she went to college. And that was an important step toward landing a serious reporting job when she graduated from college. Not the White House beat for the *Washington Post*, maybe, but a good starting job that might *lead* to the White House beat at the *Washington Post*. Followed by some time overseas covering wars and natural disasters. Then, after she'd proven herself as a serious journalist, a move to TV. Say, ABC bureau chief in Paris or Tokyo or Jerusalem. And during her spare time, she'd write steamy romance novels under a wittily chosen pen name. Only her closest friends would realize that the queen of romance and the serious, Pulitzer-prize-winning foreign correspondent were the same woman.

"Zoey?"

She snapped back to reality. "Sorry."

Mr. Schwarz smiled. "How far gone were you? *New York Times*?"

Zoey blushed. "I'd only reached the first Pulitzer prize."

"Uh-huh. Listen, this is a serious story, and she wants your best effort."

"What is it?"

"There are rumors of illegal drug use on our varsity football team. You go out with someone on the team, don't you?"

"I used to," Zoey said, feeling her heart trip.

"Are you still on speaking terms with this person?"

Zoey shrugged. "I think so. But I doubt if he'd know anything about it. Jake isn't into that at all." She hoped that was true. The night of the homecoming game Lucas had made some remark about Jake being high, but then, Lucas and Jake had never gotten along very well.

Mr. Schwarz nodded. "Still, it would give you a place to start."

"Yes, I guess it would."

"Give it your best shot. If you get a story, it could move right off the youth page onto the front page." He shook a warning finger at her. "But source everything. And triple check everything. No off-the-record quotes unless you talk to me first and clear it. This is serious stuff, and we don't want to make accusations unless we have it totally nailed down. This is not something I want you to hurry on. Take all the time you need. You understand?"

"Absolutely," Zoey said seriously. "All the time I need. Very careful." Her mind was already racing, trying to figure ways to get at the story. Ways that would bypass Jake, should it turn out that he was involved.

"Okay, take off. And don't let me down."

She turned and started off, deep in thought. Then she paused. "Mr. Schwarz?"

"Yes?"

"Thanks for giving this to me. I really appreciate it."

He winked. "Just tell me this—in the Pulitzer daydream, you're not some airhead anchor-woman, are you?"

"No way. Foreign correspondent. Trench coat and the whole thing."

She stepped out into the hallway and hurried toward her next class, practically buzzing with excitement. A real story. At least potentially a real story. Football and drugs. It would be hard to beat that combination for getting the reader's attention.

Jake McRoyan had set his alarm for four A.M. that morning. He had gotten up and pumped iron hard for forty-five minutes, working his muscles to the limit with the free weights. Then he had taken a six-mile run, circling the northern half of Chatham Island twice till his lungs were screaming and his heart was racing.

He had cooled down by viciously pummeling

the heavy bag that hung on a swivel in the corner of his room. Afterward, sweating and flushed and so weary he thought he might not be able to stand, he'd showered and, in the full-length mirror, had checked his body, flexing the muscles, looking for signs of the weakness he knew must be there.

He had let the team down. He had let himself down. He had let the memory of his brother down. All because of Claire. All because, despite the lean, layered muscle in the mirror, he was weak. And no amount of pounding the punching bag would change that essential fact.

Even Claire had at last seen it. Why else had she dumped him at the dance?

That morning he had been alone on the ferry ride over to school. Alone on the walk up the hill from the dock to school. And for the first time in his life, he had entered the school feeling that he had to avoid the gaze of the people he met.

So many people would get pleasure out of ragging on him. So many people would enjoy pointing out the hypocrisy of straight-arrow Jake, suspended from the team for refusing to take a drug test.

He had waited for it to start in gym class, his second period.

And there *had* been some banter about the lost homecoming game, but no mention of the real reason—that the star running back had been hung over through the first half, and buzzed on coke through the last half.

No one had mentioned cocaine. No one had

even hinted at his suspension. Were people feeling sorry for him? Was that it? Or had it reached the point where no one cared whether Jake McRoyan or anyone else used drugs? No. Weymouth, Maine, wasn't exactly Detroit or Chicago. Here, an accusation that a football player was using was still worth a pretty good scandal.

They ran a basketball drill in gym class, not Jake's best game, especially with sore, bunched muscles and a profound weariness from lost sleep. But although there had been one or two slams at his less-than-elegant hook shot, the dreaded word *drugs* had not been spoken.

Hell, if the situation had been reversed, *he* would have thought of plenty to say to an athlete who had blown an important game because of his own personal problems. Plenty. But there had been nothing. It was just strange.

He was leaving the locker room on his way to third period when BeeBee Hoyt fell in beside him. BeeBee was a sophomore who played tight end on the football team. Jake braced himself. Now it would start.

"Hey, Jakester. What's this I hear about you doing K-berger?"

Jake was utterly nonplussed. "What?"

"You and Louise Kronenberger, dude. After the game Friday. Is that why Claire Geiger split on you at the dance? Inquiring minds want to know."

Jake frowned. "I was at a party where she was." He concentrated. The party was a blur in his memory. It had come right after the game, right after he'd been suspended. He had drunk a great deal of beer, he remembered that. A great deal. Much later he'd managed to stagger to the water taxi and get back to the island. The next thing he'd known, he was waking up in Claire's guest room, sick and in pain.

"Tad Crowley's telling people you got faced and pranged the K-berger."

Jake hardened his expression. "Yeah, well, I guess it's open season on me now." Flashes of memory: sitting beside Louise on a couch. She had looked good. But that was all. Wasn't it?

"So, you're saying you didn't?" BeeBee pressed.

"What's it matter, BeeBee? Who the hell's going to believe anything I have to say about *anything*?" Jake demanded bitterly.

BeeBee half-closed his eyes and affected a bored look. "I don't know what you're talking about, dude," he said carefully.

"Screw you, BeeBee. You know what I'm talking about."

"No. I don't. Coach says I don't, so I don't. I'm clueless. I wasn't even there. I was in some other state."

Jake stopped and gripped the smaller boy's arm. "What are you talking about?"

Now BeeBee looked a little scared. He tried to pull away. "Chill, big Jake. Coach said it stays in the team. No one says anything to anyone about him suspending you. Ever. He doesn't want a bunch of parents on his back, I guess."

"Are you telling me no one outside the team knows about this?" Jake tightened his grip urgently.

"Coach said he'd cut the balls off the first guy who said anything. Jeez, you're breaking my arm, man."

Jake released him. He drew what felt like his first real, deep, honest breath in days. Coach was keeping things covered up. He didn't want to hurt Jake's chances of getting into a college athletics program. Plus, like BeeBee said, he probably didn't want a lot of parents running around screaming about drugs.

The secret wouldn't hold forever, though. No matter what the coach said, some guys would tell their friends, others would tell their girlfriends. But this way it would come out slowly. And dribbling out bit by bit like a piece of gossip, most people probably wouldn't believe it. After all, if anyone had a clean rep at Weymouth High, it was Jake.

"Sorry," Jake said, absently patting BeeBee's arm where he had squeezed it. "I'm a little tense, I guess." Then he shook his head in relief and amusement. "Forget that crap about me and K-berger. I'll admit I was drunk that night, but I'm not that stupid."

Jake felt a little flicker of life returning to him. A week from today he could take the drug test, pass it with flying colors, and be back on the team. He would stay sober. He would get himself back in shape. He would be up and ready for the game after next. All the crap of the last few weeks would be behind him.

Five

"This is very close to something that a human being could eat without having to run to the bathroom clutching her throat," Nina said, chewing a bite of the food from her tray. "Very close. I can't say it's good, but it doesn't make me gag."

Claire raised a skeptical eyebrow and looked across the round cafeteria table at her sister. "Are you just saying that, hoping I'll try some?" she asked.

Nina made a heart-crossing gesture. "It's honestly not awful."

Claire hesitated, waiting for either Zoey or Aisha to try a bite. Aisha obliged first.

"Huh," she said. She chewed slowly, with a thoughtful look in her eyes. "I wonder what it is?"

"It's tan, or you might prefer beige," Nina said, "with forest-green highlights that may be a type of vegetable material."

"It could be . . ." Zoey rolled her eyes to the ceiling. "I'm getting a sense of vegetables. Possibly spinach. Also, there's a hint of meat."

Claire tried it. It wasn't bad. It wasn't identi-

58

fiable, but it wasn't bad. Very likely she didn't really want to know what it was. She shrugged and had a fleeting image of an entire school being hauled away in ambulances. "So. Chances of snow in the mountains have gotten better since yesterday," she said. She focused on Zoey. "Have you asked Lucas yet?"

Zoey looked uncomfortable and began playing with a tendril of hair. "Not yet. Actually, I was starting to have doubts about the whole thing. I mean, it's such a long drive and all."

"Long drive? It's like two hundred miles, even if we stick to the highway," Claire said. "We catch the seven-forty ferry on Saturday, we load up your folks' van, and we're making our first run by noon. Ski all afternoon. All the next day. Ski the morning after that, and we're back by dinnertime on Monday."

Zoey nodded agreement but still looked unconvinced. "Well, what's this condo like?"

"Why? You suddenly need five-star accommodations? It's a nice condo. Two or three bedrooms plus a living room, a fireplace, a Jacuzzi out on the deck."

Again Zoey nodded guardedly. "So, like how many beds are there?"

Claire smiled wryly. "Oh, so that's what you're worried about. Huge surprise. Look, there are enough beds and rooms and everything that I'm sure we can work out *whatever* arrangement you want."

"It would be easier with just two bedrooms,"

Aisha weighed in. "Then it would be guys in one, girls in the other. Three bedrooms brings up other possibilities."

Claire drummed her fingers impatiently. "Look, it's not like anyone is going to have much privacy. We're not talking No-tell Motel here. I mean, if everyone comes, it will be eight people in one condo." The second the word *eight* was out of her mouth she wished she could call it back. But no one had taken any notice.

"I guess you're right," Zoey said, "but what are the guys going to think? If I go to Lucas and say, Lucas, do you want to spend a weekend in the mountains with me? he's going to think . . . you know. And lately . . . well, anyway." She started eating again, keeping her eyes down.

Claire groaned inwardly. Good grief. So Lucas was getting a little frisky. Big deal. All Zoey had to do was say no. Or yes. Or whatever.

"I know what Christopher would think if I asked *him*," Aisha said. "I mean, he'd interpret it his own way, regardless of what I said. Besides. I'm not sure I really want to spend a weekend with Christopher."

"He's living right in your own house," Claire pointed out. Why was everyone being so difficult? This should have been easy—a big group trip would make it seem only natural that Jake come along, too. After all, even though he wasn't with her anymore, he was still part of the group. And then, away from the island, with absolutely no pressure from her, the natural course of events would bring together the only two unattached people. Simple, really.

"I know he's living in my house," Aisha argued. "But so are my mother and father and my little brother. If we're all at some ski lodge, I have no one around but you guys. And anyway, that's not the only thing. I'm not even sure Christopher and I *are* Christopher and I. He has a whole different idea about how things are supposed to be than I do. At least I think he does."

"Maybe he'll come around more to your point of view," Claire said, trying to sound interested. The truth was, she didn't much care if Christopher and Aisha were together or not, except that the plan really only worked if it looked like the whole Chatham Island group was going, guys as well as girls. She certainly couldn't convince Jake to come if it was just the four girls and him. That would make it like a *girl* thing, not a *group* thing.

Aisha snorted derisively. "Christopher suffers from hound syndrome. I don't think there's a cure."

"So you guys are bailing? It's down to me and Nina?" Claire said distastefully.

"That's a horrible thought," Nina agreed. "It would end up like *The Shining*. I'd be going around saying *redrum* and she'd be chasing me through the snow with an ax."

"I could do that at home," Claire muttered. "What did Benjamin say?"

Now it was Nina's turn to look away. "I sort of forgot to mention it to him."

Claire threw up her hands. It was a clean sweep. Perfect. Now no one was going. Zoey didn't want to give Lucas the wrong impression. Aisha was trying to put distance between Christopher and her. And Nina? God knew what idea had gotten into Nina's head about Benjamin.

"Well, *I'm* still going," Claire said flatly. "By Saturday noon I will be there." *And so will the rest of you and your various boyfriends*, she vowed silently. *And Jake, too.*

Whether any of them liked it or not.

Jake's last period of the day was study hall, time he could use to go to the library, see his guidance counselor, or do homework. He had arranged his classes with a last-period study hall so he could work out in the gym and get ready for football practice. It wasn't technically an acceptable use of study hall, but no one had ever objected.

But this was to be a week without football. Which meant that study hall was . . . whatever he wanted it to be. The study hall teacher barely knew Jake's name. He was free.

It was an unusual sensation. Football had been a big part of his life ever since Wade had made the team, back when Jake was still in eighth grade. After Wade's death, Jake had followed in his footsteps. It seemed utterly strange to think that all the guys would be out on the field this afternoon, running plays without him. His first instinct was to go out and at least watch the practice. But that would have just been pathetic. And he had been pathetic enough recently.

The depressing memories crowded in on him as he escaped from history class. Drunk before a vital practice, Claire sobering him up with coffee and a shower. Drunk after the game, waking up freezing on the North Harbor dock, surrounded by the faces of his friends—some worried and sympathetic, like Zoey, others, like Lucas, barely able to conceal their disgust.

He tried to shake off the memories and walked faster. He wanted to evade Zoey and Lucas and Benjamin, who were all in the same history class. Zoey had indicated that she wanted to talk to him after class, but he had very little to say to her. She was either going to say something sweet and encouraging about his breakup with Claire, or, despite the coach's warnings, some rumor about his suspension from the team had already leaked out. Either way, he didn't want to talk to her. He had loved Zoey for a long time. Had imagined a future of them together. Her pity now, however well intentioned, would be impossible to bear.

He plowed smoothly into the anonymous hallway crowds of noisy underclassmen. A group of freshmen trying desperately to look tough were swaggering down the hall in front of him, but sensibly parted at his approach.

"Jake!"

A female voice. Jake decided to pretend he hadn't heard. It didn't sound like Zoey or Claire, but he couldn't be sure.

A soft hand touched his arm, and he had no choice but to turn and meet the person it belonged to. He fixed a scowl on his face.

"Well, you look fierce," Louise Kronenberger said, smirking at him.

Instantly he felt uneasy. BeeBee's insinuation was fresh in his mind. What were *not* fresh in his mind were the details of the party at Tad Crowley's apartment after the game. He half-tried to remember. He had a clear flash of sitting beside Louise on a couch and noticing that her skirt had ridden so far up that he could see her panties. But that was about it.

"Hi, Louise," he said, feeling something close to panic.

"Hi, Louise." She mimicked his nervous tone perfectly. "Don't want to be seen with me, huh?"

Louise glanced over her shoulder, took his hand, and drew him into a recessed doorway. She opened the door and peeked inside. Then she pulled Jake after her into the gloomy, vacant chemistry lab and closed the door behind them. To Jake's astonishment, she put her arms around his neck, raised

64

herself on tiptoes, and kissed him on the mouth.

"What was that for?" he gasped. It had been a nice kiss, but it scared him. He was wobbling on the edge of a cliff, about to lose his balance.

"That was for Friday night," she said suggestively. "I didn't want to say anything to you at the dance, what with you being there with almighty Claire Geiger." She laughed her carefree, amused laugh, a sound that struck new chords of memory in Jake's brain. Why did that laugh sound so familiar?

"I guess we had a good time Friday night," he said guardedly.

Louise made a pouting face. "You *guess*? I know I enjoyed it," she said. "Except for the times when you'd blurt out Claire's name." She erupted in another round of amusement.

Jake felt the blood draining from his face. "Louise . . . Look, I was awfully drunk that night." Plus, coming down off two rounds of cocaine, a football game, emotional depression, a suspension from the team . . .

"We were both pretty well blitzed." She peered at him closely, looking a little disappointed, as if he were a dunce stubbornly refusing to get a very funny joke. "You're not going to go into the whole regrets and second-thoughts thing, are you?"

Jake rubbed his hand over his face. It was hot and his hand was moist. "I don't know how to say this, but did something happen between

65

us? I mean, something more than flirting on the couch?"

Louise stared at him, dumbstruck. Then a slow smile began to spread. "Are you b.s.'ing me? Are you telling me you don't remember?" The grin gave way to a delighted laugh. "Your first time and you don't even remember? It *was* your first time, wasn't it? You said it was, and guys don't usually lie about how *little* experience they have."

"Are you . . . Is this true? Because, you know, it would be a pretty sick joke to play on someone."

Louise made a wry smile. She began to pull down the neck of her sweater, revealing some of her left breast. A red, puckered mark lay against the white flesh. "Want to match the hickey to the mouth?" she asked. "I'll bet it's like snowflakes, or fingerprints—no two hickeys exactly alike."

Jake rocked back on his heels. Oh God, it was true. What BeeBee had told him. It was true. Fragments of disturbing—and explicit—memory were racing across his consciousness now.

"Don't heave a kidney, Jake," Louise said. "It's not that big a deal. I mean, it wasn't *my* first time. And it was my idea as much as it was yours."

"God, Louise . . . I . . . I was so drunk that night." His breath was coming short and fast. He gulped hard. What was he supposed to say? Thanks, I'm sure I had a good time? "I didn't mean to do it. Really. I mean, that's not me. I

66

don't believe in . . . I don't know what to say."

Now Louise was looking annoyed. "Oh, grow up, Jake. I said you weren't my first. And, not that I want to break your heart or anything, but you won't be my last."

"Who have you told about this?" he demanded. Claire? Did Claire know?

She shrugged. "The people at the party had to know. Those who were sober enough to notice anything at all."

Jake shook his head despairingly. The day had begun with an unexpected reprieve, the news that Coach was covering up the drug suspension. Now it was ending with this.

What had he come to? It made him sick just to think of it. It was as if his life were spinning further and further out of control.

And worst of all was the fear that when Claire learned of this, any remote chance of their getting back together would be over.

5 Will your boyfriend say that he tells you the whole truth (A) All of the time, even if it reflects badly on him; (B) Most of the time, unless it reflects badly on you; (C) Only when it's something you need to know; (D) Only when it suits his purposes. (Try to get your boyfriend to answer at least this question honestly.)

Claire

Of all the guys I have ever known, Jake is the only one I think can honestly answer A. Possibly because he's never done anything he's ashamed of.

Benjamin will tell the truth and the whole truth . . . but only when he chooses. In other words, he's fundamentally honest, but he'll save up the truth for the time when it will do him the most good.

When I was going with Lucas, I don't know how much truth either of us ever told. He keeps his secrets. And so do I. Of course, that was two years ago. He may have changed. You'd have to ask Zoey that.

I have _not_ changed. Jake has been through some bad times lately, but I don't think he's changed, either. I'm a D and he's an A. Probably that means we're not a very good match, but I don't live my life according to magazine quizzes.

Aisha

Too easy. The answer is D. If I could get Christopher up to a C, I think I could live

with that Anything more than
that would involve transplanting
a different brain into Christopher's body. Which might not
be such a bad idea. I myself
am a B I'll tell anyone the
truth as long as it isn't something that would really hurt
their feelings For example, I do
tell Christopher he's immature
He is, he needs someone to tell
him, and anyway he thinks
it's just one of his cute character traits. I don't tell him
his singing makes birds fall
down dead out of the trees That
would hurt his feelings.

So I'm saving that for a
time when I really need to
unload on him.

Nina

I believe it was the immortal Curly who asked, "What is truth?" Or maybe it was "What is truth, nyuk, nyuk, nyuk?" Anyway, the definition of truth has haunted the great thinkers and philosophers down through the ages. Now it's my turn to deal with it, so we may start seeing some progress.

Does Benjamin tell me the truth, the whole truth, and nothing but the truth? I certainly hope not. Like I want him saying, Gee, Nina, your breath smells of Velveeta and peanut. butter, you sicken me? No. I think not. If he were an A, I don't think we'd last long as a couple. Not that we're likely to last long as a couple anyway, because I'm not sure we ever were a couple in the full sense of couplehood.

As usual with Benjamin, no single answer works. He's halfway between B and C. A C-plus, let's say. I hate to screw up his GPA like that, but maybe there will be a makeup test later.

Zoey

I think Lucas is very honest. At least about the

things that involve us as a couple. He's certainly up front about where he wants the relationship to go, and how soon he'd like it to go there. And I'm equally honest about telling him that I have a slightly different vision of the direction and speed.

Yes, I trust him to be honest. That's not the problem. The problem is when he's honest, and I'm honest, and there doesn't seem to be any way for us to agree. Then what? Either someone gives in, or both people go separate ways, or you end up like some old couple who hate each other but are staying together for the sake of the kids.

Six

Claire waited until Wednesday afternoon to act. She had been waiting for two things. First, the weather. There was no point in going ahead with what she was privately calling *The Plan* until it was certain that the weather would cooperate.

And beginning at two a.m. on Wednesday, a Canadian cold front dumped an early blanket of snow from southern Quebec to western Massachusetts. At the lower elevations it melted away, but above a thousand feet it lay across mountain slopes like a big goose-down comforter. Between this natural snowfall and the man-made snow, Killington was in business.

Second, she had waited for some evidence that Zoey and Lucas, Aisha and Christopher, and Nina and Benjamin had come back around to the idea of the road trip.

The evidence was not good. On Tuesday morning Aisha complained that now that she was spending more time under the same roof with Christopher, she was beginning to think he wasn't as good-looking as she had once thought. On Tuesday evening Benjamin had called the house wanting to speak to Nina, and Nina, who had once quivered every time Benjamin entered a room, told Claire to tell him she was out. Then, just this morning, Zoey had shown all the signs of pouting after some sort of fight with Lucas, who was showing all the signs of pouting right back.

At lunch Claire had learned that Zoey, Aisha, and Nina were going to the mall after school. They had asked her along, but she had declined.

Instead, she rode the ferry home with Lucas, Benjamin, and Jake—all three of them former boyfriends, though she hoped Jake was less *former* than the other two.

She sat down beside Benjamin. He stiffened as he recognized her and pulled the earphones off his head with a deep sigh.

"What are you listening to?" she asked.

He made a self-deprecating gesture. "Opera, believe it or not. It's the only area of music I haven't gotten into before. I'm getting so I like it. It's so extreme."

"Opera," Claire repeated. "I don't think you want to go around spreading the word that you listen to opera."

"Oh, I don't know. Maybe I'll set a new trend. A year from today, MTV might be doing blocks of opera. Pavarotti could have a whole new career as a VJ."

"Uh-huh. Have you tried any of it out on Nina?"

Benjamin smiled impishly. "You know, that was really quite subtle. I like the way you were able to work with whatever conversation was available, even opera. A very smooth segue from what you are pretending to talk about into the actual reason you came over here to sit by me."

Claire gritted her teeth. She was beginning to remember one of the reasons she'd broken up with Benjamin. "You're getting to be a suspicious person, Benjamin."

"I know. It's a serious character flaw. I'll try to do better in the future. So, what about Nina?"

"Well, I know my credentials as a big sister may be a little in doubt—"

Benjamin laughed in overly quick agreement. "—but I am still the little psycho's only sibling. And I was just wondering what you had decided about the ski trip."

A blank look. "What ski trip?"

"She didn't even tell you?" Claire tried to sound shocked. "We're all going this weekend over to Vermont. Me. Zoey and Lucas. Aisha and Christopher. And supposedly you and Nina."

Benjamin looked thoughtful. He hunched forward and began pressing his fingertips together. "Okay, I give up."

"What?"

He sat up straight. "I give up. I can't figure out what you're up to."

Claire forced an innocent laugh. Benjamin

was pound-for-pound the biggest pain in the butt around sometimes. He should think about a career with the CIA. "I'm just the one who has to make the arrangements for the condo. I want to know how many people are coming. Also, if there's some problem between you and Nina, well, she's totally inexperienced, you know, and I thought maybe I could help."

Benjamin did a double take. "You know, for a minute there I thought I heard you say you wanted to help."

Claire sighed. "Listen, Benjamin, you can think what you want about me, but I *do* care about Nina. I don't make a big thing of it, but I do care. She comes straight off the showdown with our uncle and plunges into her first big dating experience with a guy she's had a crush on for years but who, until recently, didn't even really know she was alive and treated her like his little buddy."

She was pleased to see Benjamin wince. *Take that, smart guy. I can play the guilt card as well as anyone.*

Now Benjamin looked genuinely uncomfortable. "Okay, not that I'm buying you as a concerned big sister, but the truth is I don't know what's going on with Nina and me. I thought everything was great at the dance. Then she blows me off all day Sunday. I see her on Monday and it's like she's sending signals that it was a onetime thing. She comes over and reads to me that day, but it's very stiff. And yes-

77

terday I call your house and . . . well, you were there, obviously . . . she claims she's out. You tell *me* what's going on," he ended in outright frustration.

Claire absorbed this information, none of it really surprising. "I think she's just new to all this boyfriend-girlfriend stuff," Claire said soothingly. "She doesn't know what is supposed to happen after a first date. But come on, Benjamin, she's been mooning over you for a long time."

"Maybe the reality didn't live up to the expectation," Benjamin said glumly.

"I'll feel her out. Find out what she's thinking. It's probably just nervousness and inexperience. If that's the case, do you want to go skiing with all of us?"

"Claire, just how in hell could I go skiing?" He grinned. "I'll admit it would be funny watching me try. Even better would be coming back to school afterward, telling people I'd spent the weekend skiing, and see who had the nerve to ask for an explanation."

"It's going to be a big group thing, Benjamin. You know, island kids only. It wouldn't be the group without you."

He nodded. "I'll come along for the ride. I can read and listen to music and go out with you guys at night. But I still don't get it. Eventually I will figure out what you're up to, but I have to admit, I don't see it yet."

Claire suppressed the desire to laugh in triumph. It was such a rare pleasure, manipulating Benjamin. After him, the rest would be easy. "It is remotely possible that I just like going skiing, isn't it? And that at the same time I want to see my little sister happy?"

"Yeah, right."

Claire leaned over and gave him a kiss on the cheek. "You need to lighten up, Benjamin."

The smile dropped instantly from his face as she kissed him. And, to her surprise, his reaction was not unlike her own.

Yes, there was still something there between them. But it would fade, she assured herself. It would fade.

Seven

Lucas got off the ferry and headed through the town toward his house, the image of Claire kissing Benjamin fresh in his mind. It hadn't looked like much of a kiss, more like a Hollywood *hello* kiss; still, it was the kind of thing Zoey would want him to tell her.

It was extremely annoying, the habit people seemed to have of revealing their secrets to him. Louise Kronenberger had told him at the dance about sleeping with Jake. Lucas didn't *need* to know that, didn't *want* to know that, and didn't want Zoey finding out that he knew that and somehow twisting it around to look like he was keeping things from her.

Zoey had already reamed him out over the time when he had known Christopher was getting different girls' phone numbers. Like it was Lucas's job to tell Zoey, so that Zoey could warn Aisha. Like it was Lucas's fault that Aisha had walked in on Christopher and some girl practically in the act.

And lately the secrets kept piling up and growing in importance. The worst was that he knew the idiot skinheads who had beaten up Christopher. But if he dropped a dime on the guys involved, Lucas feared they might get back at him by hurting Zoey. So he'd kept his mouth shut. Not an easy decision, or one that gave him any satisfaction. Few things would have given him as much pleasure as seeing Snake put back behind bars.

Then Christopher had asked Lucas to obtain a gun. As if Lucas knew where guns could just be picked up. As if he were crazy enough to get one for Christopher so Christopher could try to hunt down the guys who beat him up. The very guys whom Lucas was shielding so they wouldn't hurt Zoey who, if she learned any of this, would lay on a guilt trip of such epic proportions that Lucas would be left feeling like untreated sewage and no longer be allowed to kiss Zoey's foot, let alone anything else.

Yes, it would be nice to get through the rest of the year without learning any more secrets. The responsibility was too much.

He reached his house but hesitated about going inside. Yesterday his mother had told him that Christopher had called while he was out. It wasn't hard to imagine why Christopher had called. Christopher would probably keep calling. Unless he could change Christopher's mind.

With a sigh, Lucas started up the winding road that led up along the crest of the hill. It was a steep ten-minute walk to the big bed-and-breakfast. Aisha made the walk every day. The girl must have steel knees.

Kalif, Aisha's little brother, opened the door and let him in, pointing the way upstairs to Christopher's room. Lucas knocked on the door.

"Come in," Christopher said.

Lucas opened the door and his jaw dropped. Christopher was sitting on the high bed like some ancient Persian prince, propped against a mountain of brightly covered pillows, a TV remote in one hand with the other resting near an artistically arranged fruit-and-cheese platter.

"Jeez, Christopher. Do I have to bow when I come into the room?"

Christopher grinned. "You peasants are so easily impressed. Would you care for a small wedge of Brie? Perhaps a fresh strawberry?"

Lucas walked around the room and peeked into the bathroom. "Oh, man. This makes me sick. My whole room could fit in your shower."

"How is everything going down in the village?" Christopher asked. "I so enjoy hearing of the comic antics of the simple folk."

Lucas pointed to an antique-looking chair. "Can I sit in that?"

Christopher waved a magisterial hand. "Yes, I'll just have the servants clean it afterward."

Lucas sat down and looked Christopher over closely. "You seem like you're doing better."

"I am. A little stiff here and there, but I managed to do some sit-ups and push-ups this morning." He smiled at the memory. "It gave me a good excuse to lie in the Jacuzzi for an hour afterward. Actually, I'm probably eighty percent back. I'd be doing my paper route again, only I'm letting Kalif take it for a week and keep the money."

"How about your seventy other jobs?" Christopher had graduated from high school in Baltimore, moved away from his ravaged family, and set about earning enough money to go to college. He delivered papers, cooked for Zoey's father at Passmores' Restaurant, was the equipment manager for the school's athletics department, and did fix-up work everywhere around the island.

"Everyone's being very cool about it. I figure after this coming weekend, I'll be back at it. Sort of a forced vacation, here."

Lucas looked down at his hands. "Any word from the cops on the guys who jumped you?" he asked casually. If the damned cops would just catch the creeps, then Lucas's worry and guilt would be over.

Christopher's smile disappeared. His eyes, normally quick and inquisitive, went dull as steel. "No. I didn't really think there would be. Zoey wasn't able to make an identification. And I never really saw them. But I *will* see them. Sooner or later I'll find out who it was and take care of them. That's why I called your house yesterday. I still need what we talked about that night at the hospital."

Lucas shook his head. "Christopher, I don't think that's the way to go."

"Yeah? Why is that?" Christopher asked belligerently.

"Look, I spent two years in YA, and probably half the guys in there are there because they got into some revenge or payback situation. Either their parents did something they didn't like, or else their girlfriend cheated on them, or some guy didn't give them respect. I mean, payback keeps jails and prisons in business."

"So I'm just supposed to shrug it off?" Christopher bristled angrily. "Some skinhead Nazi sons of bitches try and kick my teeth in and I just go, well, too bad, let's get on with life like nothing happened? I don't think so, man. Nobody does that to me and just walks away laughing."

"Okay, fine. I can't argue with that. They ought to pay. But first, you don't even know who these guys are, and second, they didn't *kill* you, right? Justice does not say they should die for what they did."

"So I'll just injure them," Christopher sneered. "Would that be more just? I'll put them in a hospital. They can have my old room."

"With a gun? Guns are for killing. You don't *injure* someone with a nine millimeter. And what about the other thing? You don't know who these guys are. Are you just going to shoot people without even being sure they're the ones who popped you?"

"Maybe," Christopher snapped.

"Christopher, look, you and I haven't known

each other all that long, but I don't see you as being a guy who goes around just shooting people. And I'm real sure I'm not the kind of person who is going to help you get a gun."

"I can get one without you," Christopher said. "I'm over eighteen. It's legal."

"Yeah. But it would be stupid. I mean, you're supposed to go to college next year, right? You want to make it prison instead?"

"I have no choice," Christopher said in a more subdued voice. He met Lucas's eyes. "What would you do if it was you who'd been stomped in some alley?"

Lucas had expected the question, but he didn't have an easy answer. "I don't know. I guess if I knew who the guys were and for some reason the cops couldn't deal with them, I might do just what you're thinking about doing. Only you don't know who the guys are. You don't know who to go after."

Lucas could see Christopher's angry resolve beginning to disintegrate. He swallowed and looked away, and when he spoke again, Lucas was shocked and embarrassed to hear a rough trembling in his voice. "I just keep thinking if I could have got up off the ground . . ."

"Zoey said they caught you on the back of the head first. You were stunned. You were outnumbered." Lucas shrugged. "No one wins every fight. Sometimes all you can do is take your beating and try to survive."

Christopher looked like he was fighting back

tears. He bit his lip and with sudden savagery said, "Easy for you, Lucas. What beating have you ever had to just take?"

Lucas smiled a twisted, sad smile. "The one my old man gave me with his fists about twice a week until I went off to the YA." He tried to stave off the wave of anger and bitterness that rose like a volcano inside him whenever he remembered those days. "Like I said. Sometimes you just take your beating and survive."

Lucas left Christopher behind in his regal convalescence and started down the hill. It had grown dark out, and through breaks in the trees Lucas could see the brightly lit ferry gliding across unusually smooth water on its way back from Weymouth. The six thirty. It would be at the dock in another fifteen minutes, give or take. If Zoey was on it, she'd be back at her house shortly after that.

Lucas decided to wait for her there. He felt sick at heart and desperately needed some time with Zoey. She would make him forget the memory of Christopher, trying so hard to sound tough, trying to cover a fresh pain that hadn't yet begun to heal.

Watching Christopher deal with that had just brought back all the similar feelings Lucas had so often experienced. He wondered if he was doing the right thing, not turning the two skinheads over to the cops. He hoped he'd at least convinced Christopher not to go the way of a gun. But sometimes life seemed to go off into a sort of hopeless area where there were never any good answers. Just a lot of choices between bad and worse.

He paced the gravel in front of Zoey's house, growing more morose by the minute and more anxious for Zoey to come and dispel his bad mood.

"Hey, Lucas. Want to come inside and wait?"

Lucas turned and saw Benjamin, appearing to look out of his open ground-floor window. Maybe his gaze was off a point or two, but it was close. And he had *known* it was Lucas. "You're not really blind, are you, Benjamin? This is all some elaborate practical joke you've been playing."

Benjamin got the self-mocking cocky look he put on when he knew he had impressed someone. "It had to be you, Lucas. Who else would be lurking in our front yard, muttering under his breath and pacing back and forth?"

Lucas went to the door and on inside into the warmth and the light. Benjamin met him in the hallway. "You smell like potpourri," Benjamin said.

"Is that those bowls of like wood chips and stuff people leave out to smell up a room?"

"Yeah, that's the stuff."

"I've been up seeing Christopher. He's living like King Tut up there. Jacuzzi. TV. Free food. Potpourri. Real hard-core suffering."

Benjamin led the way toward the family

room. "Is he going to be able to go on this road trip, do you think?"

"A road trip?"

"You know. The big skiing weekend thing in Vermont. Everyone's going, although no one bothered to tell me until just this afternoon."

"I have no idea what you're talking about."

"Aha!" Benjamin held up a finger as if he had just made a major point.

"Aha, what?" Lucas flopped onto the couch and unzipped his jacket. Zoey's house always seemed hot. Maybe his own house was just cold.

"I don't know aha what. Yet. But I will," Benjamin said craftily. "So you're saying you don't know about the ski weekend in Vermont."

"No. Why would I be going to Vermont?"

"That's what I'd like to know," Benjamin said.

Mrs. Passmore came in, carrying a cup of coffee. Lucas liked Zoey's mother. She was about ten light-years cooler than his own mother. In fact, both of Zoey's parents were from different worlds than his own folks. And looking at Zoey's mom made him think maybe twenty years from now Zoey would still be beautiful.

"Hi, Lucas," Mrs. Passmore said. "Where's Zoey?"

"Mall day," Lucas said. "I thought she might be on the six thirty and I'd just wait here for her to get home."

"You don't need an excuse to come over," Mrs. Passmore said. "You're nicer than my own kids."

88

"Good shot, Mom." Benjamin slapped a hand over his heart. "Aren't you late getting down to the restaurant?" he asked. "We can't start the big drunken party till you leave."

"I know, I know. Never trust anyone over thirty, as we used to say many years ago."

"You're not over thirty, are you?" Lucas asked disingenuously.

"Not in dog years, maybe," Benjamin said under his breath.

"See what I have to put up with?" Mrs. Passmore asked Lucas. She checked her watch. "Actually, I am late. There's some veal stew left over from the lunch shift in the frig. You two can nuke it up if you're hungry. Bye."

"Bye, Mom."

"Bye, Mrs. Passmore." Lucas waited till she was gone. "So, are you going to explain this Vermont thing?"

"According to Claire, everyone is going to spend next weekend at this condo she's lined up. In Killington. And as part of the *everyone*, your name came up."

"You mean, like I know about this?" Lucas asked. "Like I've said I'm going?"

"Exactly. Supposedly it's me and Nina, you and Zoey, Aisha and Christopher."

"Christopher didn't say anything about it."

"See? Claire is up to something," Benjamin said thoughtfully.

"Still, it could be fun," Lucas said. *Him and Zoey*. Him and Zoey and a condo a long way from any parental types. It was hard to see where there was anything terrible in that.

Of course. That's why Zoey hadn't said anything about it.

Well, she was being kind of selfish. Just because she didn't want him to have a chance to . . . to spend some private time with her.

"Maybe it's Zoey who's up to something," he said under his breath. Oh, this was going to be excellent.

I've got you, my pretty, and your Gap bag, too. The line from *The Wizard of Oz* popped up in Lucas's mind as soon as he saw Zoey, trundling in, looking flushed from the chilly night air and carrying a bag from The Gap.

"Hi, babe." Lucas got up and took the bag from Zoey's hand and gave her a chaste kiss on the cheek.

"Hi," Zoey said, glancing at Benjamin on the couch. "What have you guys been up to?"

"We've been discussing whether quantum theory has any implications for broader epistemological questions," Benjamin said without missing a beat.

Lucas nodded agreement. "Also, we were wondering what kind of person would actually buy a Mariah Carey CD."

"I have a Mariah Carey CD."

"Yeah, but we decided you're okay anyway."

"How generous," Zoey said, sweetly sarcastic. "Come on. You can carry my bag."

Lucas followed her upstairs, barely containing his excitement. He had her. He had her good. Ms. Open and Honest. Ms. You-should-have-told-me-Christopher-was-a-hound. Ms.—

Inside the door to her room, Zoey turned and put her arms around Lucas's neck and pulled him down for a real kiss. Instantly Lucas forgot that he was supposed to be playing it cool and standoffish. Then he remembered and started to pull away, but Zoey put her tongue in his mouth and he forgot again.

"I missed you," Zoey breathed.

This was the moment for a stern, disapproving look, but instead Lucas lay back on her bed and pulled her on top. It was several moments later that the first "uh . . . uh," was sounded by Zoey, and Lucas reluctantly stopped doing what he was beginning to do.

Damn. He'd had the moral high ground and he'd given it up. Now whatever he said, he would end up sounding petulant.

Zoey gave him the consolation kiss she always bestowed after she'd flashed her STOP sign. "So what did you do this afternoon without me?" she asked.

"Went up to see Christopher."

"How is he?"

"Fine." The memory of his conversation with Christopher brought back all the guilt he'd felt at hiding secrets from Zoey. Which, in turn, brought back the justifiable outrage he felt on learning that she'd been hiding something from him.

Only he would have to be very cool. Very subtle, or he would just look like he was pouting, or else like all he was after was a chance to get her away to a private condo with a private bedroom and no parents and probably a king-sized bed or possibly a Jacuzzi out on the deck under starry skies which would get Zoey into a bathing suit . . . at most. Subtlety. That's what was required here.

"So what's this about a ski trip you didn't tell me about?" he blurted.

Zoey looked surprised and, to Lucas's infinite gratification, embarrassed. Her throat was beginning to turn red, the blush easing up into her cheeks. She looked away. "Who told you about that?"

Well. He hadn't needed subtlety after all. "Benjamin told me. Obviously you decided *not* to tell me." *Fine, now don't overdo it,* he warned himself. But it was too good to resist. "Ms. Honesty. Ms. No Secrets. Ha."

Zoey gave him an appraising look. "I suppose you think you've really got me, don't you?"

"Cold. Signed, sealed, and delivered. After all the crap you gave me over Christopher and that blond chick. After that whole honesty lecture, and how between us we'd never need secrets. There's really only one thing I can say—nah nah nah nah nah nah."

"Lucas, the reason I—"

"Nah nah nah nah nah nah. Hypocrite."

"Are we going to discuss this like intelligent people?" Zoey demanded.

Lucas held up a finger. "One more. Nah nah nah nah nah nah."

"Are you done?"

"For now," he said, holding his head at a cocky angle. "Although I reserve the right to fire another *nah* or two if necessary."

"Look. The reason I didn't mention the ski idea was that I really didn't think you'd want to go."

"Yeah, right."

"Also, *I* didn't really want to go."

"You told me you love to ski," Lucas said, shaking his head in contemptuous disbelief.

"Yeah, but *you* don't even know how to ski."

"I surf. If you can surf, you can easily learn to snowboard. You should never lie, Zoey. You are so lame at it."

Zoey took a deep breath. "Okay, you *know* the reason I didn't want to go. I didn't want you to get the wrong idea."

Here it was, Lucas realized, like a gift from God—the moment when he would get to trot out one of Zoey's favorite lines and destroy her with it.

"What you mean is, you don't trust me," he said in a sad little voice. He saw her wince. Yes! She was down. The referee had started the count.

Zoey sucked in air as if she really had been

punched. "You enjoyed that, didn't you?"

"Yes, I did."

Zoey nodded. "Well, I guess I deserved it. I was a hypocrite."

Lucas grinned beatifically. Ah, life was sweet.

"So, uh, Lucas. How would you like to drive over to Vermont this weekend?"

"Gee, I think that would be fun," he said enthusiastically. "Almost as much fun as actually winning an argument with you."

Zoey gave him a dirty look. "Enjoy it while you can. You won't be winning the argument you're hoping you'll win this weekend."

"Let's hear it one . . . more . . . time . . . Nah nah nah nah nah nah."

6 First, rate your boyfriend's looks and attractiveness on a scale of one to ten, with one being equal to, say, Senator Jesse Helms, and ten being a melding of John Kennedy Junior and Denzel Washington. Then rate yourself. Finally, have your boyfriend rate you and himself on the same scale.

Zoey

First of all, whoever wrote this quiz is showing her age. JFK Junior and Denzel Washington could practically be my dad. Dads. Well, if they were melded, one dad. A cute dad, don't get me wrong, but still a slight bit aged.

Second of all, I don't really approve of concentrating on looks as being all that important. Although I guess the point is to see whether you and your boyfriend have some wildly different numbers. Like say you think you rate a nine, but your boyfriend says you're only a four. That might be revealing, I guess.

So I'll answer, but I'm answering under protest because I don't think this is a very feminist question.

I'd give me a six and Lucas a nine.

No, I don't have a poor self-image; I'm just being realistic. I have nice hair and my face is okay, except that my eyes aren't per- fectly lined up. But I don't exactly have major breast development. Not that I'm saying a girl's self-image should be based on the size of her breasts.

I'm just saying that's one of the things society, and especially the male half of society, seems to get obsessed with.

Although why should I let society bully me into having a poor self-image? Really?

So, let me change those numbers. I'll give myself a seven. Lucas is still a nine. The only reason he isn't a ten is because I don't want him to get too full of himself.

LUCAS

Zoey's a ten. No question. I'm maybe a seven or something, especially since her previous boyfriend was Jake. That guy looks like someone from a Soloflex ad, whereas

I look more like I should
be a BASS player for some
Alternative rock band.
  But Zoey's perfect. I
mean, her face, her hair,
her legs, her . . . not to
mention her . . . whew.
Never mind. Don't want to
start thinking that way.

Claire

Oh, who cares?

Aisha

  Okay, Christopher would
say I'm an eight or a nine.
See, he wouldn't want to
insult me, but at the same
time he wouldn't want to
make me think I was too good
for him. Also he'll say he's

like an eight, maybe, although
what he believes is that he's
off the scale—a twelve or
something. Infinity.

In reality, I am probably an
eight. I think my eyes are too
far apart and also my legs are
kind of bony. Christopher, too,
is an eight. He'd be a nine or
even a ten except there's that
huge bulge in his head where he
keeps his extra ego.

Christopher

AISHA'S A NINE. I'M A TEN. THAT
PUTS ME UP BY ONE, WHICH IS FINE.
YOU NEED THAT EDGE WORKING IN
YOUR FAVOR. IF AISHA WERE A TOTAL
TEN, SHE'D PROBABLY TELL ME TO
TAKE A WALK. GIRLS GET THAT WAY
WHEN THEY'RE TOO PERFECT. LIKE

CLAIRE, FOR EXAMPLE, WHO IS A TEN
BUT WHO I WOULDN'T GO NEAR IF
YOU PAID ME.

Nina

Can we use fractions? Because
I'm just not sure I could be
accurately represented by an
integer. I feel the need for
fractions, which is odd because I
don't normally crave fractions.
Or perhaps a radical. Perhaps a
square root. Or maybe we should
employ parentheses in some way.
(Parentheses are very popular in
every math class I've ever taken,
she adds parenthetically.)

To be serious, I'd have to say

that I'm probably $\underline{x}$ squared minus y. Or the other way around.

But the real mystery is, how would Benjamin answer this question? All he can go by is what people tell him. Zoey has probably told him I'm a ten. Claire has probably told him I'm a two. That averages out to a six.

As for Benjamin, Benjamin is perfect. If Benjamin could see, he probably wouldn't have anything to do with me.

Eight

Jake slapped the alarm clock, sank back down on his pillow for a second, then forced himself up. He threw back the covers, stood up, and stumbled to his bathroom. When he came back, he began stretching out methodically: neck, shoulders, legs. He dropped to the floor and did fifty push-ups, rolled over and did fifty stomach crunches, then repeated the sequence twice more.

He had always enjoyed exercise, but it had taken on a new meaning lately. In his mind it had become the antidote to everything that had gone wrong in his life. The antidote to the depression and the inner conflict between what he saw as his duty and his fatal desire for Claire. It was the antidote to drinking and all that drinking had led to—cocaine to recover from his hangover, the loss of self-control that had gotten him kicked off the team and landed him in bed with Louise, a girl he cared nothing about.

It was a miracle he hadn't caught anything, he realized. A dose of clap or crabs would have just about topped off the week.

He looked down at himself suspiciously. So far, so good.

Jake dressed quickly in shorts, sleeveless T-shirt, and running shoes. He went out through the sliding glass door and across the patio and began running down the driveway to the road. It was still fairly dark. Not black, but a deep blue, with the moon long since gone. He ran south along the concave arc of the beach. As he turned eastward from Leeward Drive onto Pond Road he could see the horizon, already bright pink. And by the time he had joined the coast road that followed the eastern shore of the island, the brilliant crescent of the sun had peeked over the rim of the earth.

He pounded on, stride long and regular, over cracked pavement and drifting sand, arms high, his breathing not yet labored, past the shuttered, boarded-up summer homes. He could see the church spire and the familiar buildings of North Harbor, a picture of brilliant gold where the sun touched and deep night shadows that had not yet been driven off.

He ran the perimeter of the island past the Geiger house, trying but failing to stop himself from looking up and noticing that the light had not yet been turned on in Claire's room. She was still asleep, luxuriant black hair spread across her pillow, dark, serious eyes still closed.

He forced the image from his mind and accelerated the pace past the harbor, waving to the fishermen emerging from Passmores' with steaming paper cups of coffee. Zoey's father, Mr. Passmore, was standing with his own cup, dressed in kitchen whites, outside the back door of the restaurant, seemingly contemplating a spilled trash can.

Jake gave a nod and Mr. Passmore raised his cup in acknowledgment.

Another complete circuit of the island and he would have had a good workout. Down the western shore as sunlight ignited the glass and marble facades of downtown Weymouth, along the north shore of Big Bite pond past the still-sleeping homes there, up along the rugged, rocky beaches of the eastern shore.

He should turn through the town, avoiding the Geiger house altogether. But, he reasoned, it was easy to get a foot caught on the cobblestones. Safer to stick to the main road. He didn't even have to think about her as he passed. Didn't have to look. Just run and feel the slow burn in his legs and chest.

Claire saw him come past the second time. She had collected a cup of coffee from the kitchen and climbed up onto the widow's walk, as she did most mornings to watch the sun climb the sky.

She sipped the French roast and tightened the cord of her bathrobe against the breeze, a breeze that blew down from the distant and now snow-covered mountains.

Would he look up? she wondered. Yes, almost certainly. He'd be trying not to, but he would look.

He turned onto Lighthouse, moving with an easy grace that was surprising in someone so large. Claire smiled and felt a little twinge deep inside. He was such a powerful-looking creature, unstoppable, uncontrollable. He looked like he would never tire. Like he could keep running forever.

He kept his eyes firmly fixed on the road ahead, and Claire felt a momentary, perverse sense of gratification that he had proven her wrong. But then, just as he was passing by below, he turned his head and looked up, scanning up the side of the house, finding her with his eyes.

Claire sipped her coffee and gazed calmly out to sea, giving no sign that she had noticed him at all. He ran on, then looked back over his shoulder.

Well, Claire thought dryly, maybe not entirely uncontrollable.

Five blocks away, Lucas, too, was having a morning cup of coffee and enjoying the crisp air. He stood on the deck behind his house, leaning against the railing. He caught a glimpse of Jake through a gap in the buildings and trees, shook his head in amusement, and returned his closer attention to Zoey's house, just below his on the hill.

He could see straight into her kitchen and

the breakfast nook. Both were brightly lit. Mrs. Passmore was sitting with her back to him, reading a paper. From this angle he could just see Benjamin's left hand resting on the table. Zoey was in the kitchen, wearing the Boston Bruins jersey she wore to bed, white legs, and bare feet. She was fixing a bowl of cereal. She went into the breakfast nook and sat down between Benjamin and Mrs. Passmore.

Now he could see part of her face whenever she leaned forward to take a bite of cereal. One foot was curled up under her.

Lucas sighed. He felt it was somehow pathetic that he should get such profound pleasure out of watching her eat Grape-Nuts, but he couldn't help the way he felt. Seeing her this way, when he could just watch and not have to act cool, not have to exchange banter, just soak up every detail of the way she sat, the way she moved, the way God-help-him that she chewed her cereal and her tousled, uncombed blond hair lay against her neck . . .

He was disgustingly in love with her. He wanted her like he wanted life. More at times.

She laughed at something and slurped milk down her chin. She caught it with her finger and then licked the finger clean, still laughing.

"Here." Mrs. Passmore handed her daughter a paper napkin. "You still have some on your chin."

Zoey wiped her face. "I have to get going."

She took her bowl to the sink, ruffling Benjamin's hair affectionately as she passed.

She went upstairs and opened her closet door. Her eyes rested on a dress that had always been one of Jake's favorites. She was hoping to find an opportunity to approach Jake about the drug story she'd been given, and it probably wouldn't hurt to wear something he thought was attractive.

"No, Zoey," she chided herself, ashamed of the thought. That would be manipulative. If she was going to get Jake's help with the story, she'd get it honestly or not at all.

Except for the fact that *not at all* was just not an option.

She decided against the dress Jake liked and instead picked out an outfit Lucas liked.

She was climbing under the hot shower when the memory came back. A dream. Or at least a piece of a dream.

She had been skiing down a long slope. Lucas had been standing at the bottom, waiting impatiently for her. She had tried to veer off, but she found she couldn't avoid running into him. And yet it hadn't been a frightening dream. In fact, it had reminded her of flying dreams she'd had. More thrilling than scary.

That was all she remembered. Whether she'd managed in the dream to glide safely past Lucas . . . or not . . . she didn't recall. Either way, it didn't take Sigmund Freud to figure out the meaning.

She toweled off, replaced the outfit Lucas liked on the hanger beside the outfit Jake liked, and grabbed a sweater that neither of them liked.

Aisha was up, showered, and dressed earlier than usual. Which was to say that she would not have to make a mad run for the ferry. As she finished her breakfast she noticed her mother preparing a tray for Christopher. Aisha knew for a fact that Christopher was almost fully recovered and perfectly capable of coming downstairs for breakfast. But it was like some weird conspiracy between her mother, who seemed to enjoy treating Christopher like visiting royalty, and Christopher, who, of course, had no objection to breakfast in bed.

"I'll take it up," Aisha volunteered.

"It's no trouble," Mrs. Gray said cheerily.

Aisha got up from the table and lifted the tray. "He needs to start getting readjusted to real life," she said. She removed one of the two sweet rolls her mother had added and two of the four strips of bacon. "Besides, you're going to make him fat."

She carried the tray up the stairwell lined with colonial-era prints. The door of the room had a painted wooden plaque reading *Governor's Suite*. Aisha kicked the door lightly with her toe, rattling the plaque. No answer. She struggled to free a hand to open the door.

Inside, the curtains were still drawn and the room was dark. Christopher was obviously still asleep. She tiptoed over to set the tray down on the sideboard.

Aisha started to leave, but curiosity won out over good sense. She tiptoed over to the bed, nearly tripping on one of the rugs.

He was breathing heavily, his bare chest rising and falling slowly and, quite frankly, Aisha had to admit, attractively. It was impossible not to wonder what he had on beneath the quilt.

Too bad you're such a dog, Christopher, she thought. *If you weren't a two-timing, faithless weasel of a human being, you would be very, very fine.*

She leaned over and kissed him with feather-light lips. He groaned softly, but didn't open his eyes.

Was that for me, or for someone else? she wondered.

His food was going to be stone cold if he didn't wake up. Her mother would hate the idea of her food being eaten cold. Aisha leaned over him again, this time giving him a real kiss. A very real kiss.

A faint smile formed on his lips. His eyes were still closed. He moaned in a dreamy, not-yet-conscious voice. "Aisha?"

Aisha stood up and moved swiftly toward the door. When she reached it, she looked back. He was stirring, becoming conscious.

Aisha, he had said, still in his dream of being kissed. Aisha smiled in satisfaction. *Aisha,* not any other name.

That had to count for something.

Nine

The ferry pulled away, carrying Nina toward another day of the garbage disposal of the soul that was eleventh grade. She stuck a Lucky Strike in the corner of her mouth and inhaled the smell of tobacco. On the bottom of the box it said "L.S./M.F.T." She'd heard somewhere that it stood for "Lucky Strike Means Fine Tobacco." Actually, the fine tobacco stung her chapped lips. It might be wise to switch to not smoking a filtered cigarette. It might be wiser just to break the habit altogether, only as long as she didn't light up, it was harmless enough. And it annoyed so many people whom she enjoyed annoying.

Suddenly the gentle conversation beside her took a nasty turn.

"When exactly was this big decision being made?" Aisha demanded in a loud voice. "The last I heard it was a dead issue. None of us was going skiing."

Zoey was looking uncomfortable in the hideous sweater that no one, aside from her, liked. "I know, but Lucas found out about the whole thing, then it was like I was trying to hide it from him."

"You *were* trying to hide it from him," Aisha said, cocking an angry eyebrow at Zoey.

"Benjamin told Lucas," Zoey said.

Nina sat bolt upright, dropping the cigarette on her lap. "Benjamin?"

"Yeah, so actually, if anything, it's Nina's fault," Zoey said to Aisha. "She was the first to cave."

"I didn't cave anything," Nina protested. "I never said a word about any of this to Benjamin. Now he knows? He'll think I didn't want him to go."

"You *don't*," Aisha said. She was acting exasperated.

"That's not the point," Nina wailed. "It'll be like I'm dumping him or something. I don't want to dump him. I'm not even sure he's my boyfriend yet. I can't dump him in advance like that. It would be preemptive dumping. That's illegal."

"So who told Benjamin?" Zoey wondered.

"Oh, man," Aisha groaned, still giving Zoey a dirty look. "So now Claire's going, you're going with Lucas, Benjamin is probably going . . . How am I supposed to keep this from Christopher?"

"I have to ask him," Nina said, feeling panicky. "I have to ask Benjamin like it was my idea all along. I have to ask him to go and spend a *weekend* with me up on some *mountain* somewhere. And I don't even ski. I don't even like people who do ski."

111

"You could take lessons," Zoey said help-fully. "Or you could just hang out in the condo or the lodge with Benjamin."

"He doesn't even like me, I don't think," Nina said. "Now we're spending a weekend together?"

"Of course he likes you," Zoey said reassuringly.

"Did he say that?" Nina pounced greedily.

"I'm *not* going," Aisha said stubbornly.

"What did Benjamin say about me?" Nina persisted.

"He didn't say anything," Zoey said. "But you know he likes you."

Nina was far from satisfied with that answer. But what was she supposed to do? It would seem like a total slam not to ask Benjamin to go after Zoey had asked Lucas. She was trapped. Either she asked him, risking total, abject hu-miliation if he blew her off, or she didn't ask, in which case he would be hurt and think she was no longer interested in him.

And she *was* interested. Unless he *wasn't*.

She practically jumped up from the bench and made her way over to the spot where Benjamin was sitting, head back, sunglasses raised toward the sky.

"Benjamin," she said a little shrilly. "It's me, Nina."

He nodded. "Nina, you know you don't have to identify yourself to me. I know when it's you."

"Uh-huh," she said. "So. All set for the big ski trip?"

He turned his head, aiming the shades at her in his very convincing mimicry of a sighted person. "Ski trip?" he asked blankly.

What? He *didn't* know? Well, it was too late to change direction now. "Yeah, yeah. Big road trip. I figured you knew. It snowed in the mountains and like we were all going to get a condo and then Zoey and Claire can ski and the rest of us can sit around roasting marshmallows in the fireplace and take them to the hospital after they break their legs."

"Are you inviting me?" Benjamin asked.

"Of course I am. You're my . . . I mean, we're . . . you know."

"Friends?" he suggested.

It was not exactly the word Nina would have liked to hear. "Yeah. I mean, you know, Zoey asked Lucas, and I think Aisha's going to ask Christopher."

Benjamin shrugged. "Well, if everyone is going, I guess I'll go, too."

"Good," Nina said, feeling deflated. There it was again, that total lack of any of the feeling that had been there the night they'd kissed. Now it wasn't even like it had been, back when they were just good buds. "I'll tell Claire you're in."

She got up, relieved to be away from him. A feeling that did not promise much for the weekend. She found Claire downstairs, reading her Latin textbook and talking under her breath.

"You know that trip?" Nina asked without preamble.

113

Claire looked up from the book. "What about it?"

"I'm going," Nina said, feeling trapped and annoyed.

Claire nodded. "Good."

Nina did a double take. "Good?"

"Sure. Benjamin's coming, so I'm glad you're coming, too."

"Wait a minute, how do you know that Benjamin's coming?"

"I mentioned it to him yesterday and I got the impression he wanted to come."

"*You* mentioned it." *Of course. Who else?* Nina thought darkly.

"Yes. See? You say I never do you any favors. I knew you were kind of nervous about asking him, so I took care of it."

Nina's eyes narrowed in suspicion. "So you were being nice to me."

"Mmm." Claire returned to her book, but Nina caught the hint of a satisfied smile.

Nina nearly reeled from the implication. It was incredible, but there was no other reasonable explanation. Certainly not the lame explanation that Claire was trying to be nice. No. No, it was obvious what Claire was really up to.

Claire was after Benjamin. And judging from the way Benjamin had lied about his knowledge of the trip, Claire might already have been at least half-successful.

Zoey tossed the ball up over her head, drew back the racket, and brought it swiftly down. It missed the ball by six inches. The ball fell on her head and bounced off.

"Excellent serve," Aisha said.

"The sun got in my eyes," Zoey explained.

"It's overcast," Aisha pointed out. "And what kind of overcast is it?" she asked rhetorically. She raised her voice to yell down to Claire who was on the far side of the court. "Claire! What kind of clouds are these?"

"Scattered cumulus. Is one of you going to hit the ball over here at some point or can Louise and I go change?"

"I'm trying," Zoey said. She threw the ball up again and this time managed to hit it with the racket. The ball flew up and, assisted by a tailing wind, sailed over the chain link fence that surrounded the tennis courts.

"Much better," Louise Kronenberger said. "Now we don't have to play."

"One of us should go get the ball," Zoey suggested.

"Why?" Claire asked.

"Claire's right," Louise said. "Coach Androgyny isn't around. And if she comes back, we just play dumb. Tell her we thought the match ended if someone knocked the ball over the fence."

The four girls drifted toward the net, cradling their rackets and looking around warily for signs of Coach Anders. On adjoining courts, other groups of girls played on, ranging from competent to very good.

"This is so dumb," Aisha said. "Who exactly was it who had the brilliant idea to put off our gym requirement till our senior year? We could have done all this *last* year and be free right now."

"Tennis beats basketball, anyway," Louise said. "I mean, later in life we can play tennis at the country club while our husbands are off at work."

Zoey rolled her eyes. "Are you planning on doing some time travel back to the 1950s, Louise?"

"No, I'm just planning on marrying a millionaire. It's much easier than having to work and support yourself. He goes off to his office and does his job, I go off to the country club and do the tennis pro." She laughed. "Who'll be having more fun ten years from now? Me, or you—Zoey Passmore the intrepid reporter, worrying about where to put a comma in a story about the problems of the clam-shucking industry?"

"Zoey will," Claire said, unexpectedly coming to her defense. "Louise, you'll have had three brats, be living on welfare, and hanging with some guy who rides a motorcycle."

"Huh," Louise said, completely unfazed. "So what's this biker look like?"

"Like you care?" Aisha muttered under her breath.

"Actually, I am pretty open-minded." Louise smirked. "Although lately I've been trying to decide which type I like more—the big, muscular, jock type"—she gave Claire a long look—"or the

116

wiry, sensitive, bad boy." She fluttered her lashes at Zoey.

Zoey felt herself getting steamed. Louise wasn't just kidding. At the homecoming dance she'd been all over Lucas every time she got a chance. But there was no point in letting Louise see that she'd struck a nerve. Louise enjoyed getting under the skin of girls like Zoey. "The wiry, sensitive, bad boy will be spending the weekend with me at a ski lodge," she retorted.

"No! Don't tell me you're giving up your *virtue*! Not Zoey Passmore!"

Zoey felt a blush and realized too late she'd gotten teased into a pointless situation that was just going to get more embarrassing. What she should do was let it go. But with Louise mocking her, it was impossible. "No, I'm not *you*, Louise," she said. "We're all going skiing, *just* skiing. All of us together," she added.

"Oh. You mean all you virgin islanders?" Louise held up a hand. "Sorry. You're not *all* virgin islanders."

Zoey wanted to ask what she meant, but of course that was exactly what Louise wanted her to do. Besides, if Louise knew something—or thought she knew something—about one of the island kids, it was really none of Zoey's business.

Unless it was about Lucas. She narrowed her eyes in dark suspicion. Lucas had been homecoming king to Louise's queen. Had they somehow shared more than a dance?

"So, all of you are going skiing, huh?" Louise

said. She sighed. "Sounds like fun. Is your friend Christopher going, Aisha?"

Now Zoey saw Aisha's eyes growing suspicious. "I haven't decided . . . um, I mean, yes. Yes, Christopher is going. With me."

"And Jake?"

Silence. Zoey glanced at Claire, who just looked bored by the conversation. Certainly there was no sign that Claire cared one way or another about Jake. Evidently it really *was* over between the two of them. Poor Jake.

"Damn, here comes Coach," Aisha said.

The four of them wandered back toward their corners of the court.

"She was just yanking you," Aisha said to Zoey. "You know Louise—she's on a one-girl mission to spread insecurity around."

"I'll bet that's not all she spreads around," Zoey said in a voice that Louise might just be able to hear.

Ten

The idea occurred to Zoey while she was changing from gym clothes back into her normal clothes. She dismissed it as unworthy.

But during homeroom the next day the idea came back, slightly changed so that it seemed not quite so unworthy.

By lunch she had grown more used to the idea, but she had to talk to Claire about it first and Claire had not joined them for lunch.

It wasn't until her fifth-period American Literature class that Zoey saw Claire. By then Zoey had grown comfortable with the fact that her idea was partly self-serving. True, but was also a good thing to do regardless.

She was standing in the hall waiting for Claire to arrive when Jake passed by. He smiled in the distant way he'd adopted since their breakup. She smiled back, turning up the brightness level a little, and telling herself it certainly wasn't unethical to be nice to Jake.

"Hi, Jake," she said.

"Hi, Zoey," he said. "How's it going?"

"Great. How about you?"

He smiled ruefully at some private joke and said, "Couldn't be better," in a tone loaded with irony. He walked away and Zoey saw Claire approaching.

"Hey, Claire." She took Claire's arm and moved her out of the stream of traffic. "I wanted to ask you something."

Claire waited patiently.

"It's about Jake."

Claire drew a deep *why me?* breath and looked at Zoey skeptically.

"Look, I know you two just broke up and all. But you know, this whole road trip to Vermont . . . I mean, if Aisha decides to ask Christopher, and I think she probably will, you know, if she gets over being pissed off at him, well, it will be all of us. You, Nina, Eesh, me, Lucas, Benjamin, Christopher . . ."

Claire glanced toward the classroom door, clearly impatient to get into class. "So?"

"It's like everyone on the island *except* Jake," Zoey said.

Claire sighed a long, slow sigh.

"I just thought it would be nice to invite him to go, too," Zoey said. "Unlike everyone but you and me, Jake actually does ski."

Claire turned up her mouth in a faint grimace. "Are you asking my permission to invite Jake along?"

Zoey shrugged. "I just thought it would be polite to see if you minded very much."

Claire tilted her head, considering the question. "I guess it might be a little awkward, but more for him than for me. I'm just going to ski, and I don't see how his being around would keep me from skiing."

"So you don't mind?" Zoey said eagerly. The final bell rang.

"If he wants to go, I'm not going to stop him," Claire said with weary disinterest.

Zoey followed her into class and went to her desk. Jake had glanced over, but not at Zoey. His eyes had darted to Claire and then away.

Poor Jake, Zoey thought sadly. *I wonder if he knows how little Claire cares.*

It would be a good thing for him to come along to Vermont. Getting off the island and especially getting back to being part of the group would do him good. Maybe Zoey and he could patch up some of the lingering bad feelings between them. Maybe they could become friends again.

And then Zoey could ask him about the rumors of drug use on the football team. Not that that was her motivation for asking him along on the trip. No, in her heart she was sincere in wanting to reunite the group, to smooth over the rough edges that had formed in the last couple of months.

But when all that had been accomplished in a spirit of total sincerity and friendship . . . then it would be perfectly normal for her to ask for his help with her big story.

*   *   *

121

Jake spent the class paying almost no attention to what the teacher was saying. Instead he occupied his time by wondering what Zoey and Claire had been talking about out in the hallway.

That it involved him seemed certain. He was sure he had seen Zoey mouthing the word *Jake* several times. The *J* was very distinct.

Then Claire had come into the room wearing that nearly invisible smile, followed by Zoey, who had looked somewhat troubled.

Had one or both of them learned about the drug suspension? Was that secret out already? Or, worse yet perhaps, had they learned what had gone on between him and Louise?

A thrill of fear went up his spine. *They were in the same gym class with Louise!* That was it. That had to be it. That's why Claire was smirking. That had been a smirk of contempt. And Zoey had looked troubled because . . . well, just because she was nice and didn't like seeing people do dumb things.

When the bell rang at the end of class, Claire made a beeline out the door. Zoey hung back, waiting for him like a defensive lineman who was determined to keep him from running the ball.

Great. She probably wanted to talk about it. Ask him *why* and *how,* and whether he needed someone just to talk to. He steeled himself. He would handle it with dignity and honesty. Or else he'd just lie and say Louise was a dishonest slut and no way would he ever have slept with her. No matter how drunk and depressed he was.

"Jake, um, do you have a minute?"

"Sure," he said, summoning up an insouciant cheerfulness. "What's up?"

"Well, there's this idea that maybe we'd all drive to Vermont and go skiing this weekend," she said. "You know, all the old gang. Me and Nina and Lucas and Eesh and Claire and Christopher and Benjamin."

Jake nearly burst out laughing with relief. "Sounds like fun," he said.

"Anyway, it wouldn't be the group without you. So I was wondering if you'd come."

This was definitely better than getting cross-examined about Louise or his suspension. But a weekend road trip? With Zoey and Claire? And why was Zoey asking him? That was a very interesting question. He looked closely at her familiar face. Once he had been hopelessly in love with that face. It was still a very pretty face.

"I don't know," he stalled. "Where were you thinking of going? I don't think Sunday River's even open."

"We were going to go to Killington. Someone has a condo that Mr. Geiger knows or something." She waved her hand vaguely.

So. Zoey was asking him to go to Vermont for the weekend. *After* she had talked to Claire. Which meant either that Zoey had asked Claire's okay, or—aha!—Claire had asked Zoey to ask him.

Either way it could be trouble. He was *not* interested in spending time with Claire. Nor was he interested in Zoey any longer. In fact, he was getting used to being alone. Totally alone. No team, no girlfriend . . .

Just the same, though, he did enjoy skiing. And this was a *group* thing. He'd always been proud of the way the island kids tended to stick together.

"I don't have anything better to do," he said. "And if everyone else is coming, I guess I will, too."

7 How does your boyfriend feel about the other people in your life? Try to guess whether your boyfriend will say he (A) really likes; (B) somewhat likes; (C) is indifferent to; (D) somewhat *dislikes*; (E) can't stand: your closest friends, your mom and dad, your siblings, and your previous boyfriend, if applicable. Then compare your guesses to your boyfriend's actual answers.

Zoey

See? This is why I think sometimes these quizzes are a good thing. I've never really thought about how Lucas feels about all this stuff. I think for the most part that my friends are also his friends. Only to a lesser degree. For example, he likes Nina, but probably not as much as I do. Same for Aisha. I would say Lucas somewhat likes them. As for Claire, I know he doesn't trust

Claire because there's a lot
of history between those
two—most of it bad. I
won't say he can't stand
her, though. More like D,
somewhat dislikes.

He's barely talked to my
dad, but I know he likes
my mom. I think he sort
of likes the idea of my
parents. The way they're
close and work together
and are basically pretty
cool. Sometimes cooler than
I, personally, would like.
And I know Lucas really
likes Benjamin, although
it's not like the two of
them are best friends.

As for Lucas and my
previous boyfriend, Jake . . .
there's a lot of history
between those two as well.
They stay clear of each

other, mostly. Polite but not friendly. Closest to a C.

Claire

My closest friends? I guess that would be Zoey and Aisha. I don't really know how Jake feels about Aisha; more or less indifferent, I guess. As for Zoey, I'm not one of those people who think that love, once it is formed, ever really goes away entirely. I think Jake still cares for Zoey. I also think Benjamin still cares for me. I even think Lucas, deep down inside, still has affection for me. And of course I still, from time to time, have feelings of

tenderness for both of them. That's
only natural. Things aren't always
black and white. Usually they're
shades of gray.

As to Jake and my father?
Indifference. On both their parts. Jake
and Nina? There's a healthy mutual
dislike there, and always has been.

Jake and my "previous"
boyfriend? That would be Benjamin,
of course. And it's an interesting
question. Jake and Benjamin are
polar opposites. Jake is physical,
Benjamin is intellectual. Jake is
direct, Benjamin is subtle. Jake is all
about passion and duty and living out
some ideal vision of what a "man"

should be, and when he fails he's a wreck. Benjamin is brilliant, analytical, cool, with his emotions kept under such control that you wonder how long he'll be able to keep it up.

I doubt they'll ever be close.

Aisha

How can I answer any of this question? I'm not even sure how Christopher feels about me. All I can say is he <u>seems</u> to really like my mom and dad and Kalif. He <u>seems</u> to like my friends. But who knows how he likes them? For all I know, Christopher is trying to calculate some way to go after Zoey or Claire or Nina. I don't

<u>know</u>; that's the problem. I
have the feeling Christopher is
the kind of guy who would
have been happy being a pirate,
being dashing and ruthless and
always in pursuit of something
or someone.

As for previous boyfriends,
I don't have anyone who
would qualify. I went out with
other guys before, guys who
would have been happy to be
faithful to me, to be open and
honest with me, guys I could
trust. But Christopher was the
first one I ever really fell
for.

And I'm supposedly smart.
Right.

Nina

Benjamin and my best friend get along great. Of course, they are brother and sister. Benjamin and my dad get along great, too. They got to be friendly back when Benjamin was my sister's boyfriend. Benjamin and my sister? They don't get along as well as they used to, but I still have my suspicions about them. I mean, think about it. Why would Claire dump Benjamin for _Joke_? And the flip side is, why would Benjamin be happy with _me_ if he ever got the chance to get Claire back? Jeez, when I put it that way, it's enough to really make me insecure. There's only one possible solution—kill Claire in her sleep. A stake through the heart should do it, but it will have to be sometime when the sun's up and her evil power is weakest.

Eleven

After school on Friday, Zoey, along with Claire, Aisha, and Nina, went to the multistory parking garage where islanders kept their "real" cars. Real cars were the cars that were parked on the mainland. They were the usual assortment of automobiles, ranging from the Geigers' Mercedes to the Grays' more humble Taurus to the Passmores' big van, and generally came with luxuries like brakes and windshields. Unlike "island" cars, which were used only for putting around the island's few roads and were pitiful piles of junk.

They decided to take the Passmore van, since they planned to hit the mall for everything they might conceivably need on a ski trip to Vermont. But to Zoey's surprise, the van was gone from its usual space.

"One of my folks must have come over," she said, explaining the obvious.

"I'm not supposed to take my dad's car unless I clear it with him first," Nina said.

"You're not supposed to take it anyway, unless *I'm* driving," Claire pointed out.

The three of them looked at Aisha.

133

"Sure. Why not? I have the keys. Only, if I do decide to buy a pair of skis, where are we going to put them?"

"We'll strap them on top," Zoey said. "But you shouldn't *buy*. Wait and rent equipment when you get there. You may not even like skiing."

Aisha made a face. "I'll either be skiing or stuck in the condo with Christopher. I have no choice but to like it."

"You'll enjoy it," Claire said with atypical cheeriness.

They searched out Aisha's car and headed toward the mall, stereo blasting, Claire and Zoey in the back, Nina in the passenger seat in full recline mode.

"How did Christopher react when you invited him?" Zoey yelled from the backseat.

"Not as excited as I'd expected. I think he feels a little insecure about it. I mean, he's from the projects of Baltimore. Very little skiing goes on there."

"Did he ever skateboard?" Zoey asked.

Aisha shrugged. "No idea."

"Similar skills. But if he's still bruised, he might want to take it easy."

"He'll have a great time," Claire said, still eerily upbeat. Suddenly something caught Zoey's eye. She turned quickly. "Hey. There goes our van." She wrinkled her brow. She was sure she'd seen her mother behind the wheel, but there had also been a glimpse of someone beside her. It wasn't Benjamin, since he, Lucas, and Christopher had planned their own guy version of a shopping trip. And her father would be at the restaurant on a Friday evening.

She shrugged it off. She opened her purse and looked at the check register. Enough to pay for gas and for food when they got to Vermont, but not a lot left over for shopping. Unless she were to use her handy ATM card to raid her savings account, sin of sins.

There were certain things she needed. For a start, she couldn't sleep in her usual Bruins jersey. She needed something a little more substantial than that. Something substantial, but not frumpy. Somewhere about halfway between Sears and Victoria's Secret.

She took a small spiral-bound pad from her purse and jotted a note.

"What's that?" Nina asked. Reclining the way she was, her head was practically in Zoey's lap.

"My list."

"You and your lists," Nina said, mocking her.

"Hey," Aisha said. "Don't make fun of lists. I have a list. If I didn't keep lists, I'd never get anything done."

Nina slapped her forehead. "So *that's* why I never accomplish anything. I remember once I'd been planning to find a cure for cancer, only I never wrote it down on a list. Sure enough, I forgot."

"So what's on your list?" Aisha called back over her shoulder.

"Oh, the usual. Little sample bottles of

shampoo and conditioner so I don't have to carry big bottles."

"I have that, too," Aisha said.

"Me too," Nina added. "In my head. My head list."

"Actually, this is just a small part of my bigger list, which is the list of stuff to bring with me tomorrow," Zoey admitted. "Clothes, makeup, and all that."

"Black lace teddy?" Nina asked.

"No. In fact, I was going to shop for something warm. Flannel, maybe."

"You could get pajamas with feet in them, like when you were little," Nina suggested. "That would stop Lucas dead in his tracks."

"This is not about Lucas," Zoey said. "It's about staying warm. We don't know how well heated this condo is, or if there are enough blankets."

"Or enough beds," Nina said with a leer.

Zoey grabbed Nina's jacket and placed it over Nina's head.

"It's a fully stocked condo," Claire said reassuringly.

"So you think we'll see the guys at the mall?" Aisha wondered.

"If we do, it will only be for a brief moment as they race past in perfectly straight lines, buy whatever they came for, and take off," Zoey said. "You know how guys shop. Speed shopping."

"That's because they never buy anything," Nina said, her voice muffled under her coat.

"Whereas I"—she produced a gold American Express card—"have the power to buy anything I want."

"Where did you get that?" Claire demanded.

"I asked Dad for it," Nina said, pulling her jacket off her face. "I told him I was thinking about changing my look entirely. I showed him a picture from a J. Crew catalog. You know, all clean and preppy looking. Sort of a blazer-chinos-pennyloafers look." She laughed. "Out came the old Am Ex."

"That's very devious," Claire said. "I'm proud of you. And as long as I get to use it, too, I won't even tell Dad how you manipulated him."

Trip Purchases: The Girls

Zoey

1 flower print flannel nightgown (JC Penny's)
1 3-pack of cotton underwear (JC Penny's)
1 R.E.M. CD
2 pairs L.L. Bean heavy woolen socks
1 pair ski pants
1 blue satin nightshirt (Victoria's Secret)
1 Swiss army knife
3 books: *First and Forever, Fireworks,* and *Sweet Savage Love*
2 rolls 35-millimeter film
1 sample-size shampoo
1 5-pack of razor blades
1 ChapStick

Claire

1 pair ski boots
2 pairs ski pants
1 leather miniskirt (Filene's)
1 wool-blend sweater (The Limited)
2 pairs L.L. Bean heavy woolen socks
1 sample-size shampoo
1 pound French roast coffee
2 books: *Amo, Amas, Amat and More* and *The Last Wilderness*
1 ChapStick

Aisha

2 books: *Skiing for Beginners* and *The New Guide to Skiing*
3 pairs L.L. Bean heavy woolen socks
1 pair gloves
1 Ace bandage
1 bottle Advil
1 pair ski pants
1 pair green satin pajamas (Filene's)
1 sample-size shampoo
1 sample-size conditioner
1 sample-size Crest
1 small loofah sponge
2 magazines: *Ski* with article on Killington and *Mademoiselle* with article "Why Men Lie"

Nina

1 Porno for Pyros CD
1 large bag peanut M&M's
2 pairs men's boxer shorts
4 pairs L.L. Bean heavy woolen socks
1 Barney the Dinosaur mask (Spencer's Gifts)
1 sample-size Afta Shave
3 temporary tattoos
1 Thighmaster
1 ChapStick

Trip Purchases: The Guys

Jake

1 new binding
1 pair new poles
1 pair sunglasses
1 hand-grip exerciser
1 bottle Afta Shave
1 ChapStick

Christopher

2 books: *Skiing for Beginners* and *The New
    Guide to Skiing*
1 pair gloves
1 bottle Listerine
1 bottle Safari cologne
1 box Trojan sensi-ribbed condoms

Benjamin

3 CDs: B.B. King, Blind Melon, and Mozart
2 books on tape: *A Morning for Flamingos*
  and *The Wine-Dark Sea*
1 scarf (hopefully black)
1 bag Jolly Rancher watermelon candy

Lucas

1 bottle Scope
2 Tic-tacs
1 box Mentor condoms

Twelve

Zoey and the girls returned to Chatham Island on the last ferry and arrived back at nine twenty-five. Zoey said good-bye to her friends and went straight to the restaurant. It was Friday, and with Christopher not available to pick up shifts yet, both her parents would be working late.

Her father was in the kitchen, cleaning it up after the evening dinner business, leaving out only what he would need to send the occasional order of steamed shrimp or nachos out to the bar.

"Hi, Dad," she said, setting her several bags of purchases on the stainless steel counter. She gave him a kiss on the cheek.

Mr. Passmore wore his hair pulled back in a ponytail fastened with a twist tie from a bread bag. He wore a faded Albert Einstein T-shirt under a food-stained white apron. He was nursing a cup of coffee to one side, while he stretched plastic wrap over a steel tub full of what looked like soup.

"No one on this island appreciates a good gumbo," he said. "Lobstah, steamahs, sometimes a good chowdah," he said, mimicking the Maine accent.

"So, you guys will be eating gumbo all weekend, I guess," Zoey said.

"What, you won't eat it, either? Oh, yeah. I forgot. The big road trip." He smiled. "Brings back memories of when I was your age and the road trips we used to take. Three of us drove from Dayton to Santa Fe in two days because we heard you could get peyote legally." He made a face. "Which is probably *not* the story I should have been telling you."

"We're just going skiing, Dad."

"Cool. But your mother wants to have a little talk with you."

Zoey let her shoulders sag expressively. "No drinking and driving, no drugs, no picking up hitchhikers—like there would be any room."

"Yeah, all that," her father agreed. "And my fatherly addition—if the red oil-pressure light goes on in the van—"

"Pull over immediately."

"Mmm. How much money do you have?"

"Well, I just went shopping."

Her father dug in his pants pocket and pulled out a handful of cash. "Looks like fifty-three dollars. Here. And don't tell your mom I gave you any. That way she'll give you some out of the register."

Zoey went out through the swinging doors into the dining room. She said hello to the waitress and found her mother behind the bar, waiting on half a dozen people.

"Dad said you wanted to give me a lecture before I took off," Zoey said.

"Well, you're not going now, are you?"

"First thing tomorrow morning. We're going to catch the seven forty. I figure you guys will still be asleep."

"Good guess." Her mother surveyed her customers. "Anyone ready? Tom?" When she got only negatives, she pulled Zoey aside into a corner of the dining room. They sat down at one of the tables.

"I just want to get a few things out on the table before you take off," her mother said.

"No drunk driving, no shooting heroin, no hitchhikers, and if the little red oil light comes on, I just keep driving till the van burns up."

"I know you know all that, Zoey, but I'm serious. No one drives drunk. Not you, not anyone. Even just one beer, you don't touch the key. Are we totally clear on that?"

"Mom, do you even realize that I don't drink?" Zoey asked.

"You don't? Ever?"

"I've had one or two beers in my whole life."

"Wow," her mother said. "I mean, that's good."

"I'm not the kind of person who would do something dumb like drive halfway across the country looking for peyote," Zoey said, batting her eyes.

Her mother nodded. "I know you're not. Anyway, just because *we* were stupid when we were young doesn't mean we're going to put up with *you* being stupid." She looked down at the tablecloth, picking at a spot of dried-on food with her fingernail. "Are you sleeping with Lucas?"

Zoey rolled her eyes and fervently wished she could just slip quietly from the room. She shifted position in her chair. "No, *Mother*. Of course not."

"Well, that's good," her mother said without much conviction. "I mean it really is. It was different when I was your age. All we had were crabs and clap and syphilis. We didn't have venereal diseases that were fatal at all, let alone a hundred percent fatal. Hell, we didn't even have herpes. At least I never heard anything about it, let alone AIDS. Man."

"Is that all you wanted to tell me?" Zoey said hopefully.

"Look, I'm just saying that if for any reason you *do* decide to sleep with anyone, use condoms."

Zoey felt the heat in her face, but with luck, in the dimly lit room the blush wouldn't be noticeable. "Mother, I know all that."

Her mother reached across the table and laid her hand on Zoey's arm. "Of course you do. But I'm telling you again because I want you to remember. I know it sounds like I'm being a hypocrite, but the truth is I'd be happier if you didn't start having sex at all yet. I can't control what you do or don't do, I know that. So, all I'm saying is, *if* you decide to do it, use a damned condom because that way at least you greatly *reduce* the odds of catching anything *and* the odds that I'm going to become a grandmother."

"Yes, Mother," Zoey said, gritting her teeth. "By the way, did you give this same lecture to Benjamin?"

"No, your father took care of that. After I twisted his arm a few times."

"Oh." Zoey was disappointed. She'd been hoping to at least catch her mother being sexist. "Anything else?"

"Yes. When you use a public toilet, flush it with your foot and don't sit all the way down."

Zoey smiled. "Got it."

Her mother looked at her and shook her head a little wistfully. "You're a good kid, Zoey. I don't know how your father and I ever managed to have two such great kids."

"Benjamin and I can't figure it out, either," Zoey said. "Hey, I saw you driving around when I was on my way to the mall. Who was with you?"

Her mother's eyes flickered. Then she shrugged indifferently. "There wasn't anyone with me."

"I thought maybe it was a hitchhiker," Zoey said accusingly.

Her mother made a face. "Go on, get out of here. Take some money from the register. And have fun. Just not too much."

Zoey lay in her bed, looking up at the low, sloping ceiling. She should get some sleep because she would have to do at least some of the driving tomorrow and she hated driving with a lot of people in the car. She had a vivid imagination and always conjured up images of driving into a train, killing or injuring everyone but herself. That way she would have to be alive and healthy and go around visiting all the people she had hurt in the hospital.

She wondered how Claire dealt with knowing that she had been driving and was responsible, at least in large part, for the death of Wade McRoyan. She herself would never have been able to handle the guilt. But Claire was a different person than she was. Everyone was different.

Like in the way they dealt with guys—Claire, always so in charge and in control, dumping one, grabbing another. Like the way she had just blown off Jake with hardly a second thought.

Claire was like Louise Kronenberger that way—always cool, no matter what.

Although there were some big differences. Like, for example, Zoey was pretty sure Claire had never done it.

She smiled up at the dark ceiling. That's because guys were too scared of Claire to ask.

Unfortunately, Zoey did not seem to have the knack of being in control. She couldn't be imperious like Claire. And she certainly wasn't going to be easy like Louise.

What had Louise meant with that crack about not all of them being virgin islanders? Had she meant Lucas?

Zoey shifted onto her side and pushed down the covers. Suddenly she was hot. The dreamy, philosophical mood had evaporated. Sex, sex, sex. It was like there was some huge conspiracy—Lucas, pushing and pleading and practically begging; her own mother, ready to hand her a box of condoms; every magazine on the stands, with one article or another about better sex, or more sex, or different sex.

The whole world wanted her to have sex. Even *she* wanted herself to have sex a lot of the time. It would make Lucas so happy and so grateful. And it wasn't like there weren't times when she thought about it, and even played out various scenarios in her mind. Just doing it would put an end to the whole battle of wills between her and Lucas.

But she had experienced many of these same thoughts when she had been going with Jake. Jake had been no more subtle than Lucas. And back then she had thought about how it might be fun with Jake, and how happy he would be, and grateful, and how it would put an end to the test of wills.

She loved Lucas. She felt she loved Lucas even more than she had once loved Jake. And yet, what if she had slept with Jake and then they'd broken up? And what if, somehow, some way, she and Lucas ended up breaking up?

She shifted onto her other side and looked out the dormered window to see silver moonlight on the bare branches of the trees. Tomorrow morning—or maybe it was technically morning already—she was going off, for the first time, on a weekend trip, more or less alone with a guy. A guy she loved, who loved her. Only he wanted the love to be physical.

And the only question was, in the end, should she say yes or no?

*   *   *

A few blocks away, Claire was also awake. But when she'd realized she wasn't falling asleep, she had pulled on a warm parka and climbed up to the widow's walk. With chilly fingers she'd reached around the brick chimney to the one loose brick, pried it out, and found her diary. She huddled with her back against the railing and tilted the pages toward the light of the moon. Reading was impossible, but she could see well enough to write in a straight line.

Temperature: 41 degrees. Almost no wind. Clear.

Tomorrow is the big ski trip. My plan has worked so far. Jake will be there alone. I'll be there alone. I'm hoping that a week of solitude and believing he's lost me will help him get past all the stuff that's happened between us.

And then what? True love and

happiness? I have no idea. I'd like to think so, but I have to take things one step at a time. First, get Jake back. Then decide what that means for the longer term. Tomorrow's the big day. I've never gone away with a guy before. Although having six other people along keeps it from being a honeymoon exactly. I'm a little nervous about it all. Surprising, since there's really nothing to be nervous about.

Claire closed the diary and slid the pencil back in the spine. Nothing at all to be nervous about. Except, if Jake still rejected her, it would mean . . . being alone, but that didn't bother her.

It would mean that he hadn't forgiven her. That she still wasn't free of a night not unlike this one, two years earlier.

8 Will your boyfriend say it is okay for him to (A) look at other girls as long as it is totally innocent; (B) look at other girls, deliberately make eye contact, and smile; (C) look at other girls as much as he wants as long as he doesn't actually ask them out; or (D) never look at other girls when he's with you.

Nina

Okay, next question.

Zoey

I guess I don't mind it when Lucas looks at other girls. Just looks. If he was like Christopher, looking with serious intent, getting phone numbers and all, then I'd be very upset. And I think Lucas and I are in agreement on this. I think he'll answer A. If he answers B or C, I'd be kind of not all that thrilled. But I'm not so insecure I'd want him to answer D. I guess that would be asking too much.

Although I never look at other guys when I'm with Lucas. Almost never.

Claire

I'm not bothered by guys looking at other girls. I look at other guys, so it's only fair that I should extend that same right to Jake. Besides, I'm not the kind of person to get all worked up into an insecure, jealous frenzy like a lot of girls. Either there's nothing to worry about, in which case it's a waste of mental

energy, or there is. And if there is,
then the relationship is over anyway.

Aisha

I wouldn't mind guys looking at other girls if they could
at least do it with a little subtlety. You know, like the way
we girls look at guys: quick,
discreet, yet comprehensive
With guys it's like they're
trying to memorize everything
when they look at a girl Like
they want to be able to remember every tiny detail later on
Personally, I don't even want
to think about why they're
that way, but they are
Now, Christopher would say
he's free to look all he wants

<u>and</u> go get the girl's number
Which is why I'm not so
sure I should even be taking
this quiz, because I'm not so
sure I have a boyfriend But
as for just looking, that's no
big thing

   Wait a minute Yes, it is I
can't lie It pisses me off

   It PISSES me off Only I
can't do anything about it

   Yet

Thirteen

THE DRIVE

Weymouth

From Weymouth to Portland, Zoey drove and Nina took the front passenger seat. In the second row of seats, Aisha sat beside Christopher who sat beside Claire, who was wearing the leather mini she had purchased the day before. In the cramped space, her leg was pressed against Christopher's leg. Aisha was annoyed. Christopher glanced several times at Claire's legs, annoying Aisha still more.

Lucas, Jake, and Benjamin all sat in the far back, their shoulders cramped together. Lucas and Jake looked out their windows in opposite directions, having very little to say to each other.

Nina controlled the stereo and played the Porno for Pyros CD she'd bought the day before. This got on Benjamin's nerves because he was sitting back by the speakers. It also annoyed Zoey, who hated driving with other people in the car. One wrong turn could lead to a lifetime of guilt and regret.

Outside Portland, Nina insisted they make a pee stop at a McDonald's.

From Portland to Portsmouth, New Hampshire, Claire drove. Zoey moved to the back, thinking it would put her with Lucas, but when Lucas came back from the McDonald's, he grabbed the relatively roomy front passenger seat. So Zoey ended up sitting between Benjamin and Jake.

Aisha and Christopher were still together, with Nina beside Christopher. Nina was wearing faded, baggy pants and boots, and Christopher showed no signs of looking at her legs. So Aisha relaxed. Until she realized that Christopher could, from his angle, look up at the rearview mirror and get a fairly scandalous view of Claire's legs.

Claire, however, was using the rearview mirror herself, to watch what looked like Zoey and Jake in friendly conversation. Lucas ate an Egg McMuffin and channel-surfed the radio endlessly, driving everyone crazy.

Nina wondered darkly if Claire's frequent glances in the rearview mirror were aimed at Benjamin.

In Portsmouth they lost their way trying

to find Highway 4, resulting in a babble of helpful and conflicting suggestions that drove Claire, as soon as she had finally found the right road, to pull into a 7-Eleven and demand that someone else drive.

From Portsmouth to Concord, Jake drove, always a competitive event for him. He played highway tag with a car from Massachusetts, at one point rolling down the driver-side window to tell the other guy he was, in the phrase Mainers reserved for drivers from Massachusetts, a *Mass*-hole.

Benjamin sat in the passenger seat and, out of sheer perversity, played an opera CD until a group vote that he be forced to stop.

Nina, Zoey, and Aisha sat in the middle seat. Claire was in the back, sandwiched tightly between Christopher and Lucas, a situation that annoyed Jake, Aisha, and Zoey simultaneously. Snappish behavior began to break out all around, with arguments over music, how much the windows should be open or closed, heat, and driving style.

Nina suggested they should all join together and have a sing-along. She launched immediately into the Barney theme song, in which no one else joined.

Just past Concord, Aisha made a pee stop request, but Jake refused to stop. Zoey joined in the pee stop request. Benjamin, who was grumpy over the defeat of his opera, backed Jake. Nina joined Aisha and Zoey. Christopher lined up with the other guys and an argument on bladder differences between the sexes and its meaning in the world of sports, the military, and big business ensued.

At last Claire spoke up, told Jake in her quietly authoritative voice to pull over at the next rest stop, and he did.

Aisha drove from the rest stop to Lebanon, climbing into altitudes where snow clung to tree limbs and many of the cars were carrying full ski racks. Jake got the passenger seat. He turned to a rock station that faded in and out.

Christopher ended up in the far back with Zoey and Lucas. Lucas and Zoey held hands beneath the jacket draped over his lap. Christopher wished he could hold hands with Aisha, but Aisha was driving and, anyway, they didn't seem to be getting along all that well.

In the middle seat, Benjamin was stuck between Nina and Claire. Nina calculated the degree to which he was in contact with her versus the degree to which he was in contact with Claire. It *seemed* he was sitting closer to Nina, but there was no way of telling what was going on in his head. He might be paying much more attention to the contact with Claire.

They hit another McDonald's in Lebanon and Nina took over driving duties, because while no one had much faith in her driving, no one stepped forward to tell her so. Zoey took the seat beside her, watched the map, and clutched the dashboard fearfully each time Nina turned around to talk to someone in the back. The landscape had grown whiter all around as they climbed ever higher, but the roads remained clear.

Now Claire was in the middle seat next to Jake, both of them carefully ignoring each other, though Claire let her skirt creep up her thigh and Jake kept leaning forward to rub his forehead in a way that let him glance at her and then hate himself for glancing.

Benjamin sat behind Nina, wondering why she seemed to smell of Afta Shave.

Aisha was in the backseat, not objecting to the fact that Christopher had made room for his shoulders by putting his arm around hers.

Lucas sat on the other side of Aisha, trying not to notice Claire's hair, draped back over her seat so that it fell across his knees.

By the time the van pulled parked in front of the cluster of wood-frame, two-story condominiums, everyone was exhausted.

Killington

159

Fourteen

Claire breathed a sigh of relief as she surveyed the condo. They had made it. They were here. The Plan was working. And Jake had been mooning over her all the way up in the van. Except for that brief period when he'd seemed to be enjoying talking to Zoey.

The condo looked great. Upstairs were two bedrooms joined by a balcony that overlooked the tiny village of Killington. The downstairs featured a huge living room, a kitchen, and a second long deck with a redwood hot tub. From the deck the view was straight up the side of the mountain, a vast, rising expanse of frosted fir trees crisscrossed by dozens of white ski runs and the little red daisy chains of gondolas, looking like Christmas ornaments.

Zoey came up behind Claire and grabbed her arm as she was admiring the view. "There are only two bedrooms," she hissed in an urgent whisper.

"There's a fold-out couch there in the living room," Claire pointed out. "One bedroom has two double beds, and the other has one double. Altogether, with the couch, that's sleeping for eight people. What did you want? Bunk beds?"

"How are we going to divide up?"

Claire shrugged impatiently. "I assume it will be girls with girls and guys with guys. At least, *I* don't have any more exciting plans."

"Well, neither do I," Zoey said.

"Fine, so what's the problem? You share with Nina, I'll share with Aisha. Great. Now, let's get changed and hit the slope. I want to get back in shape quick. Before we leave, I want to be ready to try a black diamond trail."

"You're on your own, then," Zoey said. Trails were ranked in order of difficulty from green circle to blue square to black diamond. *Double* diamond trails were for professional-level skiers or the suicidal. "You're no better a skier than I am."

"Hey." Lucas, looking unsure of himself with hands in pockets, accompanied by Christopher. Benjamin had found a La-Z-Boy and had it in full recline. "Everyone's wondering where we should put our stuff," Lucas said.

"We figured guys sleep with guys, girls with girls," Claire said confidently.

Lucas and Christopher exchanged a shocked look and shuddered visibly. "Sleep with a guy?" Christopher said. "Not in this lifetime."

"You're just sharing a bed," Claire said.

"Who's sharing a bed?" Jake asked, arriving and slinging his bag onto the couch.

"Me and Nina," Zoey said, "Claire and Eesh. Then you guys work out whatever arrangements you want."

"Wait a minute," Jake said. "Like I'm going to be *in the same bed* as Christopher or Lucas? In what universe?"

"What's the problem?" Claire demanded. "*We're* sharing beds."

"You're girls," Lucas said. "Guys don't sleep with other guys."

Zoey gave him a dirty look. "Well, you can forget the other alternative."

"So can *you*," Aisha told Christopher in the same tone of voice.

"That's not what this is about," Lucas grumbled.

"Uh-huh."

"Right. There's some *other* reason," Aisha said. "You guys cooked this up together, didn't you?"

"Actually," Benjamin said, speaking for the first time, "it's just something that guys don't do. We don't wear pink. We don't use the word *cute*. And we don't sleep with each other. We're manly men."

Claire felt herself doing a slow burn. What was the matter with all these people? She was trying to set up a nice romantic weekend here and get in some skiing, and between Zoey's outraged chastity and the guys' terror of homosexuality, they couldn't get past stage one.

"Look. Here it is," she said. "Two of you guys have to volunteer to sleep on the floor."

"So *all* the girls get beds, but only half the guys," Jake summarized. "Nice try."

"Jake," Claire said, striving to keep her voice mellow, "the girls are willing to share, two to a bed. You guys *won't* share, so two of you get beds and the other two get six feet of carpet."

Jake shook his head. "Uh-uh. We all draw straws or cut cards or something. Four people get beds. Four get floor."

Aisha planted her hands on her hips. "I'm not sleeping on the floor just because you insecure males are terrified you might wake up in the night and discover that your hand is accidentally on another guy's butt."

Bad tactic, Claire realized. Very bad tactic. All four guys had looked panicked by that mental picture.

"Look," Zoey said. "It's you guys who are the problem here. If you'd share beds, we could *all* have beds."

"*We* are not the ones with the problem," Lucas pointed out. "See, maybe it's you girls with the problem. After all, you're the ones who won't share a bed with a *guy.*"

Christopher gave Lucas a high five, but Claire noticed that neither Jake nor Benjamin joined in.

"Fine," Claire snapped. "Let's draw lots or whatever. Four people win. Then those four people can invite or not invite one of the remaining four to share. For my part, if I win, I'll sleep with Zoey or Aisha."

Nina chose that moment to come wandering in from the bathroom. "Excuse me? Claire? Is there something you've been hiding from me all these years?"

"Let me have your pack of cigarettes," Claire demanded.

163

"Smoking *and* sleeping with girls?" Nina asked archly. "Boy, you sure change when you get away from home."

Claire snatched the pack from the pocket of Nina's jacket. She extracted eight cigarettes, ignoring Nina's protest. She broke four of them in half, throwing away the excess, leaving her with four long and four short cigarettes.

"You know, you could have done that with just six cigarettes," Aisha pointed out. "Four long, break the other two in half and use both halves."

"Thanks for that math update. Here. Choose. Long gets a bed. Short gets floor. I'd like to get up the mountain sometime before next month." She stuck the cigarettes out toward Jake. He pulled a long one.

In quick succession Nina, Lucas, and Christopher pulled long ones.

"Unbelievable," Zoey complained, staring at her short cigarette. "Three out of the four guys. That means two of the girls are on the floor. What are the odds?"

"Arrangements could be made for some lucky girls," Christopher said with a leer.

"What do you mean, *two* girls are on the floor?" Nina demanded. "I count three."

"One of the girls can sleep with you," Zoey explained. "Namely, me."

"Ha. I don't think so. I won fair and square. Besides, I contributed the cigarettes. You losers are on your own."

The seemingly endless bed debate had been followed by a nearly as long bed*room* debate, with tempers, particularly Claire's, flaring. To Benjamin, she seemed once again to have some hidden agenda that she was impatient to pursue. But then again, maybe she just wanted to hit the slopes.

Finally, Benjamin found himself on the lower deck listening to the receding crunch of boots on snow, the voices growing fainter with distance. He trailed a finger through the hot water of the tub and felt the icy breeze on his face. He felt he could sense the awesome weight of the mountain towering above them. Could imagine the detail, filling in remembered colors, almost as if he were painting a picture. It might not be identical to the reality, but it was a good picture anyway.

Then he heard someone coming through the sliding glass doors, stepping out onto the deck. Nina. He should have realized that Nina hadn't left with the others. Instantly his mood darkened. She was trying to be nice, of course, but he didn't want her to be nice.

All the others had gone. The three confirmed skiers, Zoey, Claire, and Jake, had headed off at last to the lifts. Lucas, Christopher, and Aisha had gone off to sign up for either snowboarding or skiing lessons, figuring to try whichever was easier. Nina had stayed behind to be *nice*. The word for that kind of nice was *pity*.

Damn it, if anyone should know better, it was Nina. She knew him well enough. But maybe now that their relationship had changed, she was no longer ready to give him the rough, egalitarian treatment that he appreciated from her.

He didn't mind the being left behind. The simple fact was that there were limits on what a person could do without being able to see. He would never be an airline pilot, he would never be a marine rifleman, and he would never be a serious skier. Being the person he was, he wasn't thrilled about having to close off possibilities, but he had adjusted. He dealt with it without self-pity.

But other people inevitably felt sorry for him. Felt they had to find ways of including him in things. And it was that pity that burned.

"What are you still doing here?" he asked as gently as he could manage.

"I don't ski," she said simply. He could hear her climbing up to look down into the hot tub.

"Neither does Aisha. You could learn, though." Nina was trying to be nice, he reminded himself.

"I'm not all that into physical stuff. I mean, I can barely dance, as you know."

"You dance fine," he said tersely. Surely she should be getting the message by now.

"That doesn't mean I can ski. Besides, I'd rather just hang—"

"Look, Nina," he snapped suddenly, "I'm a big boy. I can amuse myself. I don't need a baby-sitter."

He heard her sharp intake of breath. What surprised him was the prolonged silence that followed it. As it stretched on it became more unsettling. Was she looking at him? Ignoring him?

At long last, "Screw you, Benjamin." A voice with tears in it.

"Nina, I'm not trying to be a jerk, but I don't need you to hold my hand for me."

"Yeah? You know what, Benjamin? Just because you're cranky from the drive up here, and just because you wish you'd never gone out with me, that doesn't give you the right to dump on me."

"Wait a minute, what are you ranting about? This is about you feeling sorry for me because I can't go and ski."

"No, that's *not* what it's about. I know better than to ever show anything like pity for The Great Benjamin Passmore, Sightless Wonder Boy."

"Fine, then you understand. So go off and enjoy yourself."

"You know, you're right. I was under the stupid impression that I might enjoy myself by being with you. But that was before I realized what a jerk you are."

He heard the door slide open.

"You said whatever happened, we'd always still be friends, Benjamin. But all it took to put an end to that was one lousy kiss. Yeah, one *lousy* kiss!" He heard the door slam, and then the ringing emptiness of the vast open spaces.

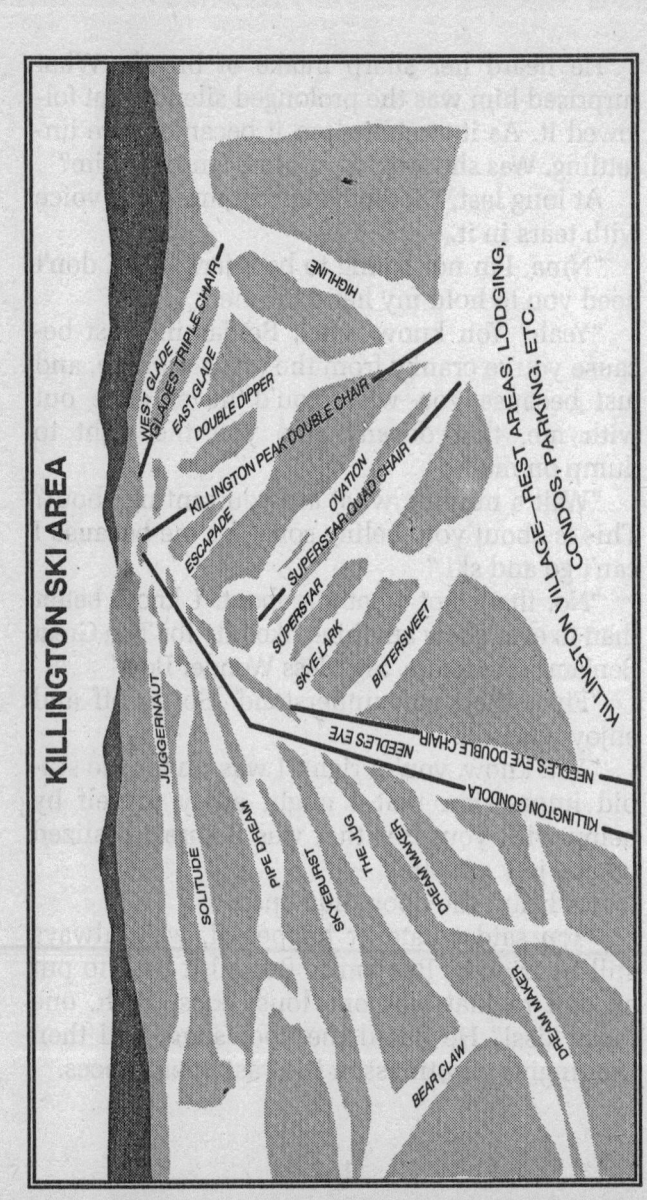

KILLINGTON SKI AREA

HIGHLINE
WEST GLADE
GLADES TRIPLE CHAIR
EAST GLADE
DOUBLE DIPPER
KILLINGTON PEAK DOUBLE CHAIR
ESCAPADE
OVATION
SUPERSTAR QUAD CHAIR
SUPERSTAR
JUGGERNAUT
SKYE LARK
BITTERSWEET
SOLITUDE
PIPE DREAM
SKYEBURST
THE JUG
DREAM MAKER
NEEDLE'S EYE DOUBLE CHAIR
NEEDLE'S EYE
KILLINGTON GONDOLA
KILLINGTON VILLAGE—REST AREAS, LODGING, CONDOS, PARKING, ETC.
BEAR CLAW
DREAM MAKER

Fifteen

Claire felt the familiar rush of anticipation as
the chairlift scooped them up, lifting their skis
free of the snow, holding them in a careless grip
as it drew them up the side of the mountain,
swaying and wobbling high above the skiers
below. It was an environment in which she felt
so at home—cold, clear, quiet. Private, except
for Zoey alongside her on the two-person chair.

They rose over birch and fir trees whose
branches drooped under the weight of snow.
And as they rose the panorama expanded, wid-
ening out across a dozen rounded mountain
peaks, blazing sun winking and dancing along
the wide white avenues of ski runs. Back down
the mountain, the cars in the parking lot, the
base lodge, the pristine village had all been re-
duced to Matchbox toys, or some too-perfect-to-
be-realistic model.

Ahead a few dozen feet was Jake, ignoring
the other person sharing his chair.

Claire allowed herself a moment of smugness. By the end of this day the group would
have broken down into its component couples.

Zoey would have found a place to be with Lucas, Aisha with Christopher, Nina with Benjamin. Only Claire and Jake would be wandering alone, unattached. But with a hot tub, a clear starry night, a fireplace, the warm, mellow afterglow of a day on the slopes . . .

It was a pity to have to manipulate him this way, but it was his own fault for being stubborn. She loved him, he loved her. Just because he seemed determined to screw that up didn't mean she had to let him.

They reached the top after a fourteen-minute ride. Claire readied herself, slipping her gloved hands through the straps of her poles. Ahead Jake was obviously not waiting around to be friendly. He was already making his way toward the head of a trail, weaving confidently around other skiers. Claire muttered under her breath.

"What?" Zoey said.

"I said, there he goes." She grinned. "Race you to the bottom, Passmore."

Before Zoey could answer, Claire launched herself in pursuit of Jake. Jake had always been a more powerful skier, but Claire had greater finesse. She thought she could probably catch him, even pass him. If neither of them took a spill first.

Jake was schussing straight down the fall line, gathering speed down the particularly steep early part of the trail. Claire dropped into a tuck position and went after him.

The suddenness of acceleration took her breath away, literally, and it occurred to her that

170

she hadn't skied in seven months, that she was badly out of shape, out of practice, and trying to chase a guy with unbreakable knees down a challenging trail. The smart thing would be to take her time, get readjusted, get warmed up, practice a few moves, and *then* get serious.

But Jake was getting serious *now*. It had become a challenge. Jake was trying to get away. And she wasn't going to let him.

They were halfway down the slope when she saw Jake lose it in a mogul field, making a wrong turn that sent him tumbling. She laughed out loud, a sound instantly snatched away by the wind. That would teach him to be a hotdog.

Should she stop and help him retrieve the loose ski that had escaped into the trees, or just coolly fly on by with a superior smile? Or maybe the best thing—

She felt something wrong. Felt the skis flying out from under her. Hit hard on her right shoulder, rolled, twisted, skidded, slid out of control on her behind, tried to dig in her heels, misjudged, flipped forward, and came to a final halt with her head buried in the snow, limbs splayed.

She pulled her head up and spit compacted snow out of her mouth. Snow was packed behind her sunglasses, and she cleared it with her clumsy gloved fingers. And a healthy handful of snow was down her back, out of reach. She would just have to wait for it to melt.

"Are you okay?" Jake, sitting just a few feet away, leaning back against a birch tree.

"Aside from feeling like an idiot? Yeah."

Jake went back to reseating his boot in the binding of his runaway ski. "You know, you're not actually supposed to stop by using your face that way."

Claire was crawling forward to retrieve her own skis, which had stopped in the trough of a mogul. "Go ahead and laugh," she said sourly.

Jake grinned. "I think I will. I mean, that was a bad fall. I thought you might have snapped your neck. But then I realized you were just demonstrating the new 'ostrich' stop, where you stop by suddenly sticking your entire head into the snow."

Claire laughed despite herself. "I was trying to beat you to the bottom."

"I might have been showing off," Jake admitted. "And it was going pretty well there up until I went airborne."

"Oh, great," Claire said. "Look at this." Zoey was gliding calmly past in a shallow traverse, giving a nonchalant wave. She yelled something and grinned.

"What did she say?" Jake asked.

"'Tortoise and the Hare,'" Claire said. "You know, the kids' story about the race between the rabbit and the turtle, where the turtle wins because she doesn't try to show off when she's totally out of shape?"

Jake used his poles to push himself up. He came over and, after planting himself firmly, gave Claire a hand up.

"You know, if we cut across here we can catch

a nice, gentle trail," Jake suggested, sounding almost shy.

"After you, tortoise," Claire said happily.

It was going better and faster than Claire had hoped. She had spent the afternoon skiing with Jake. Sometimes they ran into Zoey, but without any spoken agreement or acknowledgment between them, Claire and Jake had become partners for the day. Riding the lifts together, always staying within sight of each other, challenging each other with stunts that rarely ever worked.

But she was aware that it was a shaky truce. She had caught him watching her admiringly from time to time, but that didn't mean much. The question had never been whether Jake was attracted to her. The question was whether he was ready to let go of the past and get on with living his own life.

In other words, to do what she wanted him to do.

By the time the sun began to drop below the peaks, they were both worn out and chilled. They spotted Zoey a distance away, heading toward the ski school, and caught up with her.

"Hi," Zoey said. "You two champions do any more of that trick skiing you were demonstrating earlier?"

Claire gave her a dubious look. "I suppose you didn't fall once."

"Not more than six or eight times," Zoey said. "Never face first though. I prefer the popular butt fall. Let me ask you this—are your shins killing you?"

"You need to lean against the front of your boot more," Jake suggested. "I always used to tell you . . ." He let the sentence drift away. Claire knew he'd been the one who'd taught Zoey to ski. They'd gone fairly often, back when they were boyfriend and girlfriend, sometimes with Jake's parents, once or twice with the Passmores.

"You were a great teacher," Zoey said sincerely. "I was lucky to have you."

Had there been an emotional subtext there of some kind? Claire wondered. Probably not. Zoey had a low threshold of subtlety. She was just being nice, telling Jake that she was still his friend. And that was good. Probably.

They came to the base of the novice slope and Zoey shielded her eyes, looking around for Lucas.

"There's Aisha and Christopher," Claire said, pointing. Christopher was sidestepping stiffly up a gentle rise while Aisha was snowplowing down, looking nervous about moving at just over walking speed.

"Let's race over and make them feel like rank, pathetic amateurs," Jake suggested, grinning wickedly.

"That would be rude," Zoey said. "Let's do it."

The three of them got up what speed they could and stopped just short of Aisha, throwing up as much snow spray as possible.

"Show-offs," Aisha muttered.

Christopher schussed woodenly down toward them, unable to stop until he was several feet past them. He looked back over his shoulder. "So this is what white people do for a good time, huh?"

Jake shrugged. "There has to be at least one sport white people are better at."

"For now," Christopher said. "Let me get a few more lessons and then we'll see. So far, all I know how to do really well is fall down."

"You'd have a long way to go before you could fall any better than Claire did," Jake said with a laugh.

Claire slapped his arm with her glove. "You went first."

"Where's Lucas?" Zoey asked.

"He just left a little while ago," Aisha said.

"Oh. He didn't like it?"

"Huh. He went nuts. He decided to do snowboarding and he's just been crazy. It's like he found religion or something. Bouncing around on those humpy things—" She made a wavy motion with her hand.

"Moguls," Zoey supplied.

"I think he wore himself out. He took off for the condo to thaw out his feet."

"Which is just what I'd like to do," Christopher said. "I'm not totally back up to a hundred percent . . ."

"Excuses, excuses," Aisha teased him.

"Let's all head back. Thaw out, then go see about food and nocturnal entertainment," Jake suggested.

"Nocturnal entertainment?" Christopher repeated, adding an exaggerated lascivious leer.

"Absolutely," Aisha said with a wink at Claire. "Too bad you're not a hundred percent, though. I couldn't be very entertained by a guy who was just, what, seventy percent?"

"There's a club for kids who don't have fake IDs," Jake said. "It's usually full of freshman scrotes, but we could just ignore them. And the music is okay."

"We're there," Claire said. A little music, a little dancing. Yes, she was truly a genius. It was all going like clockwork.

Sixteen

They arrived back at the condo, laughing and teasing, and ran into a stony wall of bad temper. Benjamin was in the living room doing the frostily polite routine Claire remembered well. She guessed it was possible Benjamin felt left out of the day's activities, but that wasn't like him at all. He knew what this was going to be like. It was more likely that he was pissed off by Nirvana, pounding from the floor above.

Claire went upstairs and found Nina, listening to her CD boom box and looking like a storm cloud. Nina glanced up at her resentfully and went back to reading a magazine.

Claire peeled off her ski clothes and began digging in her bag for something warm and soft. She found a heavy gray felt bathrobe and slipped into it gratefully. "Have a good time today?" she asked Nina.

Nina's response was a sneer. *Okay,* Claire thought, *trouble in paradise.* She went over and turned the music down to a more reasonable level.

"Turn it back up," Nina snapped.

"Nina, not that I want to sound like Dad, but

there are other people around, and other people next door, too."

"What, did *Benjamin* ask you to come up here and turn down the music?"

"No, actually Benjamin didn't have much to say."

"He had plenty to say to me," Nina grumbled.

"I'm guessing there was a . . . disagreement?"

"No. No disagreement. We agree. We agree totally."

Claire sighed. Her muscles ached and various parts of her body were tender and bruised. Plus, the familiar cold-induced lethargy had begun to steal over her, making her dopey and thick. "Why don't you two work it out? I'm going to go jump in the shower."

She headed for the bathroom.

"I have nothing to talk about with that weasel! Maybe *you* should talk to him, Claire!" Nina shouted after her.

Ten minutes later, feeling somewhat more alert, Claire went back to check on Nina. Not that she cared about Nina's spat with Benjamin, but she did want to keep things running along smoothly.

But back in the room she found Nina deep in passionate conversation with Zoey and Aisha. Zoey was interrupting every few minutes to say, "Look, I can't get between you and my brother."

Aisha was listening impatiently. "So why don't you just grab him, sit him down, and say hey, what the hell is the deal with you, Benjamin? Cut to the chase."

"Oh, like you do with Christopher?" Nina pointed out.

"That's different," Aisha claimed. "Benjamin's easy to talk to."

"You know something? I'm tired of hearing about what a saint Benjamin is," Nina said. "Everyone thinks he's perfect. But I'll tell you, he can be pretty snotty when he wants to be. And rude. And mean, too."

"Benjamin, mean?" Zoey asked disbelievingly. Then she held up her hands. "Sorry. I'm not involved."

"He should just come right out and say—" Nina suspended her sentence when she realized that Claire was in the room. "Never mind."

Claire sighed and slipped out of her robe.

Nina gave her a dirty look. "And I wonder why Benjamin isn't really interested in me," she said pointedly. "He's still pining for the lost ice princess and her twin icebergs."

Claire pulled a sweater on over her head. "Leave me out of it, Nina. This sounds like it's between you and Benjamin."

Nina looked away, obviously embarrassed by having come right out and been vocal about her jealousy. "Yeah, right," she muttered.

Claire pulled on pants and a pair of new socks. "Nina, why don't you just go and apologize to Benjamin for whatever idiotic or annoying thing you did to make him mad. Tell him it's just the way you are, that you're somehow genetically programmed to be a pain in the ass. He'll believe that. I know *I* do."

Lord, she thought as she headed down the stairs. *You try to arrange a simple little seduction and it has to turn into a three-ring circus.*

Aisha felt slightly ridiculous, standing in front of a sliding glass door just inches from darkness and below-freezing temperatures when she was wearing nothing but a bathing suit. But she couldn't wear a parka into the hot tub and, having never experienced a hot tub outside, and being sore from a day of skiing lessons, she was determined to make the run.

The only question was shoes. It was only about five steps to the tub, but the wooden deck was covered with tracked, dirty slush. The problem was, if she put on shoes to run to the tub, she would have to pause to take off the shoes, and that would leave her exposed, bare flesh to the wind for extra seconds.

"Go for it, Aisha," Lucas said, leaning over her shoulder to look out. "I'd join you, but I'm afraid Zoey and Christopher might both get the wrong idea."

"It's cold out there. Normally I don't wear a bathing suit when it's twenty degrees."

"Soon as you hit the water you'll be fine," Lucas assured her.

Aisha took a deep breath and slid open the door. "AHHHHH!"

She ran on tiptoes, scampered up the side,

180

and plunged neck deep into the steaming, churning water.

Lucas stuck his head out the door. "Of course, what I forgot to mention was that the real problem comes when you decide to get out." He gave a smile and went back inside.

Get out. Yes, Aisha realized, that could be painful. Still, for now it was heaven. She moved weightlessly around the tub until she located a strategically placed jet. Ah, yes. This *was* good for the tired muscles.

She leaned her head back against the side and looked off toward the mountain. Night had fallen, but the moon was still trapped behind the mountainside, backlighting the peak with a silvery luminescence. Overhead were more stars than Aisha had ever seen before, sharp and unblinking in the crystal mountain air.

A steady foot traffic moved from the nearby condos toward the base lodge and other restaurants and night spots. A group of middle-aged types in bright down parkas came walking past and gave her a friendly, mittened wave. She raised a hand from the warm water to wave back but instantly lowered it again. Yes, getting *out* would be the tough part. She might just have to stay in here forever.

She heard boots crunching on snow and pried open one eye to look. It was a guy following the same path as the middle-aged group, only this one was much younger. He smiled as he drew near.

"Is good night for this thing, yes?"

Aisha smiled, partly because she was just feeling good, and partly because his accent was sort of sweetly comical. "It's a beautiful night, yes."

He stopped and looked over the railing at her. "I am Pyotr. Peter."

"Aisha," she said. He seemed harmless enough, and she didn't want to be rude to a foreigner.

"Isha?"

"Aisha," she repeated her name more slowly.

"Peter," he said. "But in my country, Pyotr."

"Nice to meet you," Aisha said. It was a strange circumstance for meeting someone for the first time, but Pyotr-Peter seemed nice and was definitely cute, accent or no. He couldn't be more than eighteen or nineteen, she estimated. "What country are you from?"

"Estonia."

"Oh." She had no clear idea where Estonia was, but had the sense that it was in Europe somewhere. "Well, nice to meet you, Pyotr."

"Very pleasant meeting you also, Aisha. Shall you be going to a club or disco, I hope?"

"A little later, maybe," she said.

"Then if I have the luck, I will see you later." He smiled and headed off down the path toward the lodge.

Estonia. Now where on earth was Estonia? And what was a very cute Estonian doing in Vermont?

The glass door slid open and Christopher stuck out his head. "Why didn't you tell me you were coming out here? I would have joined you."

She cocked a finger at him. "You've just answered your own question."

"Funny. Come on, we're all going to get something to eat."

"I can't get out," she said.

Christopher's face lit up. "You mean you're . . . you don't have any clothes on?"

Aisha rolled her eyes. "Little one-track minds," she muttered under her breath. Were guys in Estonia like this? Probably not. They probably spent all their time wondering where on earth they were. "Actually, no, Christopher, I don't have anything on. And I'll get out, but I want you to close your eyes and not peek."

"Okay," he said quickly. "No problem."

"You *swear*?"

"Cross my heart. Jeez, Aisha, I'm not some slimeball."

"Okay. If you swear. Close your eyes."

He did, covering them with his hand. Aisha stood up and dashed toward the door, dripping water that would be ice in a matter of seconds.

"You have a bathing suit on, you liar!" Christopher yelled in outrage.

Aisha ran past him and jumped inside. "How would you know, since you swore not to look?" She left him to think of an answer, slid the door shut on him, and threw the lock.

9 Will your boyfriend say that his dreams about you are usually rated G, PG, PG-13, R, or X? How about your dreams of him?

Zoey

Okay, who wrote this stupid quiz? I mean, I know it's a quiz for girl-friends and their boy-friends, but honestly, with some of these questions I don't even want to know the answers. And I certainly don't want Lucas knowing all of _my_ answers.

I think dreams are pri-vate. What your subcon-scious comes up with isn't something you should be telling people about. Really. It's just not anyone else's busi-ness. Not even Lucas's business.

Besides, I don't think dreams mean anything. Just because in a dream maybe you're . . . well, never mind. It's no one's business.

LUCAS

There is a very useful saying I learned while I was in jail—I respectfully refuse to answer on grounds that it may incriminate me.

Aisha

I think dreams are out of your control, so they tend to be about a lot of different things, all mixed together Sometimes a person shows up in your dream and it's like he's just part of the crowd Other times, maybe he's the star player But if you averaged them out, I guess my dreams wouldn't rate anything more than a PG No biggie There aren't any demons hiding in some dark corner of my brain

As for Christopher's dreams, I hate to think I guess, being realistic, that I do show up there sometimes in his subconscious Sometimes I may just be the UPS delivery driver or something Other times, who knows? Who wants to know?

Okay, I'd like to know But not if he knew that I knew That would be sick

Christopher

THE TRUTH IS, I VERY RARELY

REMEMBER MY DREAMS. THE ONES I DO REMEMBER ARE USUALLY MORE LIKE NIGHTMARES, AND WITH THOSE I'D JUST AS SOON FORGET.

THE GOOD ONES FADE AS SOON AS I OPEN MY EYES, WHICH IS A DRAG. I THINK IT WOULD BE COOL TO BE ABLE TO HAVE REALLY GREAT, OUT-THERE DREAMS—MAYBE A SPORTS ILLUSTRATED SWIMSUIT EDITION MEETS THE FORBES LIST OF THE 400 RICHEST PEOPLE AND I'M AROUND NUMBER SIX ON THE LIST AND MOVING UP DREAM. COME TO THINK OF IT, THAT'S MY MOST FREQUENT DAYDREAM.

ANYWAY, I HOPE I'M HAVING GREAT R- AND X-RATED DREAMS BECAUSE I'D LIKE TO THINK THE OLD SUBCONSCIOUS IS HAVING A REALLY GOOD TIME, EVEN IF I'M NOT.

Nina

My dreams are all about fuzzy bunny rabbits. I believe that Benjamin also dreams about fuzzy bunny rabbits. Now is this quiz over with yet?

Okay, honestly, I used to have recurring nightmares. They were about what happened with my uncle, and they were not fun. I have them less now, but occasionally they'll still come bubbling up out of my subconscious. They're rated D for disgusting.

But I'll bet Benjamin has really cool dreams. I doubt that I'm in any of them, except maybe as a minor supporting actor. You know, like I could be the person watching helplessly as he falls . . . falls . . . FAAAAALLS! Aiyee!

But if he did happen to dream about me, I think it would be like a G-rated thing. You know, okay to see with your parents. Bring the kids. When he dreams of Claire, it's probably more like a PG-13, you know, but for sheer horror, not for sex.

BENJAMIN

In my dreams I can often see. Sometimes I can "see" people I've never seen in real life, people I didn't ~~nkow~~ know back then. Or I see these people changed, grown older or something. Sometimes these visions are so extraordinarily compelling that I can't help but believe them. I've "seen" Zoey this way, older than I remember her from when we were little and I was still sighted. I've seen Claire and Nina, too. All of them—Zoey, Claire, Nina—are very beautiful in my dreams. Maybe they're beautiful in real life, too. Or maybe I just have an artistic and optimistic subconscious.

But I don't have R-rated dreams, ~~tle~~ let alone X, because I'm simply too decent and mature and gentlemanly a guy for that.

And if you believe that . . .

Claire

There are a lot of storms in my dreams. Tornadoes and hurricanes and thunder. I'd love to see a real tornado someday. Be as close as I could get, hear it and feel it . . . I find those dreams very exciting. But they're G rated. And those are about the only dreams I remember. Sometimes a dream about my mom, but those are just sad. Sorry. Nothing very exciting here.

As for Jake? He probably dreams about football.

JAKE

I have two kinds of dreams—R-rated dreams, which make me kind of spacey all the next day, and football dreams, where I can't make my legs run and the defensive linemen are all huge brutes who are going to crush me into the dirt and stomp me with their cleats.

Mostly I prefer the R-rated dreams.

Seventeen

Full of burgers and potato skins and nachos, they arrived at the club. Nina had been expecting the worst. She figured that an underage club in a ski area would be playing a mix of weenie tunes. And in her present mood, a single Michael Bolton song could cause her to run amok. Instead, they walked into a good sound system with Aerosmith blowing through "Big Ten Inch Record."

"Good sign," Nina said. The first good thing to happen all day long.

"What?" Zoey yelled, cupping her ear.

"I said, thank God they're not playing the kind of stuff *you* like."

Zoey gave her a nasty look but decided against a comeback. Nina was near the edge and creeping closer all the time.

Lucas took Zoey's arm and led her away toward the dance floor. Aisha and Christopher followed them. Claire spotted a booth just emptying out and made a dash toward it.

A group of younger kids arrived at the booth at the same time, prepared to put up a fight. But then Jake went up, jerked a thumb over his shoulder, and the younger kids slunk away.

"You're such a big bully," Claire told Jake. "It's very useful."

They sat down, Nina separated from Benjamin, who ended up on the far side, sitting beside Claire. *Coincidence?* Nina wondered. *Yeah, right.* She didn't believe in coincidence where either Claire or Benjamin was concerned.

Suddenly she felt depressed. Maybe it was the music, which had shifted into a bluesy Robert Cray song. The lyrics were all about mistrust— *". . . but I suspect foul play . . . I suspect foul play."*

Oh, yes. She suspected foul play, all right. She suspected the whole reason behind this stupid trip was to give Claire an excuse to be with Benjamin.

". . . sitting here and thinking back, it all starts making sense . . ."

Claire nudged Benjamin's shoulder and whispered something in his ear. At first he looked a little confused, or even embarrassed, but he slid out of the booth and let Claire lead him to the dance floor.

Nina followed them with her eyes. Oh, yes, maybe you could say hey, no big deal. Why shouldn't they have a dance? People danced with other people without it meaning anything. Out on the dance floor, Zoey was now dancing with Christopher and Lucas with Aisha. No biggie. Except that again, with Claire and Benjamin, nothing was ever innocent, no matter how innocent it looked.

Nina glanced at Jake. He looked like he was arguing with himself. His eyebrows twitched from time to time, and his mouth even moved in muttered, unheard conversation.

Suddenly he looked over at Nina. His expression showed a half-formed, unwilling intention to ask her to dance. Nina shook her head no and Jake looked relieved.

The song ended and segued into some Pearl Jam. Zoey went over and danced with her brother. Christopher headed off to the rest room and Aisha came over and grabbed Jake, who went along meekly.

Claire sat down at the booth and took a long drink of her soda without acknowledging Nina.

Nina realized she was boiling. She'd been pissed off at Benjamin all day long. After storming out of the condo she'd wandered around the village, bored, which had just made her more resentful. Then, at dinner, when Claire had actually fed Benjamin one of her French fries, she'd gotten really steamed. Now she was so angry that she was unable to keep still, leg bouncing, hands drumming the tabletop. It probably just looked like she was responding to the music, but that wasn't it. Eddie Vedder's anger was just feeding her own, giving it shape.

It was a strange feeling. An unknown feeling. Not that Nina had never been mad before. But she had never been this kind of mad. There was a new element added, something desperate. Something that twisted her insides.

Not just anger. She knew anger. For years she had denied her anger at her uncle. Had denied her anger at her father for putting her in the position of being used by her uncle. Denied, especially, her unjustified but still real anger at her mother for having died.

No, not just anger. It was jealousy, Nina had to admit. That was the feeling. Rotten, soul-chewing jealousy.

Claire had had her chance. Nina had waited and hidden and suppressed her feelings for Benjamin for all sorts of reasons: from fear, from self-loathing, from guilt. But at last, she had gotten past some of that stuff, *enough* of that stuff that she had taken the huge emotional chance of telling Benjamin how she felt about him.

She had gone to homecoming with him and basically announced to the world that she was no longer the person everyone had known. She'd crossed the damned bridge, taken the risk, *kissed* him! And now . . . now it was like it all had never happened. Benjamin couldn't even seem to stand having her around. And Claire was the cause. She was certain of that. At least *part* of the cause.

"What did you and Benjamin talk about?" Nina demanded. The sound of her own voice surprised her.

Claire cocked a disdainful eyebrow at her. "Am I supposed to report to you?"

"I just want to know what happened."

"No."

"Damn you, Claire."

Claire looked surprised. It was dawning on her that this time her little sister wasn't just playing around. "What is the matter with you? Having a PMS attack?"

Nina's hand was trembling as she lifted her Coke to take a drink. There was no point, she told herself. She couldn't win a fight with Claire. And she didn't want to fight. What was she fighting *for*? For a guy who'd kissed her exactly once and then blown her off? The reasonable thing to do was just—

Only she wasn't feeling reasonable. "I know you're after Benjamin. I know that's what this whole stupid trip is about. You think you're so damned smart, Claire, but I know you set this all up."

Now Claire looked alarmed. She shot a glance toward Jake, returning with the others to the booth. Claire bit her lip, cursed under her breath, and quickly slid out of the booth.

"Running away, Claire?" Nina snapped.

Claire whirled. "I don't want to have a family fight in front of everyone. Outside."

Nina hesitated only a moment. All right. They'd do it outside. She jumped up and brushed past Zoey, ignoring her greeting.

Outside, the air was still and shockingly cold. Claire was waiting in the parking lot, arms crossed over her chest, looking, in the unnatural bluish lights, like Morticia in a bad mood. The bass from the music filtered out from the club but seemed to leave undisturbed the more profound, underlying silence.

"You want to run that by me again?" Claire said.

"You know what I said. You set this whole weekend thing up so you could go after Benjamin. I know you're still in love with him and you won't let him go. You think you're so brilliant, but I caught you, Claire. I figured out your game."

Claire pointed a finger. "Nina, I think you should calm down."

"I don't want to calm down!" Nina cried, her voice suddenly ragged.

"Look, you need to get a grip." Claire's voice had dropped to a low, deliberate calm. "This is kind of new to you, I know. The whole boyfriend-girlfriend thing. And you are overreacting."

"I am not," Nina said. Tears filled her eyes. "I'm not stupid, you know. I know Benjamin likes you better. Everyone likes you better. Big surprise. But I really—" Her voice choked.

Claire moved closer. Nina turned away, defeated and humiliated by the tears that were flowing freely.

"You're wrong about people liking me better," Claire said. "You're wrong about everything you just said, and what you suspect."

"Forget it," Nina muttered.

"Look, Nina, here's the truth. Of course there is still something between Benjamin and me. Yes, I still look at him and think he's attractive. And, yes, I guess . . . no, I *know* he hasn't completely forgotten his feelings for me."

"At least you're being honest," Nina said in a tired voice.

"Things don't just end cleanly and completely between people who've been in love."

Nina nodded. "Yeah, well, it's not like I can compete with you. You decided to get him back; what the hell can I do?"

"I did not decide to get him back," Claire said.

Nina risked a glance at Claire's face. She looked annoyed. Annoyed was Claire's version of sincere.

Claire sighed and glanced back toward the door of the club. "Okay, I'll tell you, Nina. But for once in your life, you keep your mouth shut. I mean *shut*." She sighed again. "I didn't set up this weekend to get back with Benjamin. I set it up to get back with Jake."

Nina frowned. "You just broke up with Jake."

"Well . . . Look, he was all bent because he thought by being with me he was forgetting about Wade. And since I seemed to be trying to force him to forgive me, he'd gotten himself backed into sort of an emotional corner. You understand?"

Nina nodded, although she was mystified.

"So I dumped him. That way I knew he'd start missing me. Human nature—you can reject what's easily available, but you always want what you can't have."

"So . . . you pretended to dump him. You acted like you couldn't care less, and he—"

"He realizes what he's missing, finds a way to make peace with himself, and then, all that's necessary is"—she held out her hands, encompassing the dark mountains, the starry sky, the warm light of the village—"the right time and place. And with a loud popping sound he'll pull his head out of his butt."

Nina digested the information and felt the pieces falling into place. "You *were* flirting with Benjamin . . . but only to make Jake feel insecure."

"Very good, Grasshopper," Claire said sarcastically.

"Oh, you *are* rotten." Nina laughed suddenly. It was breathtaking. "You're more manipulative than even I ever realized."

Claire smiled her infrequent smile. Naturally, she thought Nina had just complimented her. "See, it's about me and Jake. Not about me and Benjamin. Although I will say one thing." Her voice softened and the smile grew wistful. "You picked a good guy to fall in love with when you picked Benjamin."

Nina nodded mutely. "I just don't think it goes both ways."

"You're on your own with that, little sister. The only advice I can give you is—think about getting your own head out of your butt and telling him how you feel. Be direct."

"*Direct?* Why? You aren't."

"I'm me. You're you," Claire said with weary condescension. "You have to work with what you have.

Eighteen

Aisha had danced a few dances with Christopher and one with Jake, just because she felt like dancing and he was available at the moment. Then she'd danced with Benjamin and Lucas, being democratic about it. Then, feeling guilty because she'd neglected Christopher, she went looking for him.

She found him holding court, telling a small group of kids, a guy and two girls, a story about Baltimore. Looking more closely, she saw that one of the girls was wearing a silk Baltimore Orioles baseball cap. It went well with her tissue-paper-sheer top and long, bare, presumably cold legs. Possibly it was all just innocent talk about Christopher's old hometown, she told herself. Only Ms. Orioles kept touching Christopher's arm whenever she asked a question.

Yet she didn't want to go stomping up like THE GIRLFRIEND, acting all proprietary about Christopher. Especially since they weren't even officially boyfriend and girlfriend.

"Hi. Is me, Peter. You recall?"

Aisha turned and saw him smiling at her.

The dorky hat he'd been wearing was gone and so was the parka. Definite improvements.

"Estonia, right?"

He smiled, showing a nice lineup of pearly whites. "Do you enjoy to dance?"

"Sometimes."

"Maybe you have a boyfriend?" he asked tentatively.

"Funny you should ask," Aisha said. She glanced at Christopher, who was leaning in to hear something Ms. Baseball had to say. "If you're asking me to dance, the answer is yes."

They danced two songs. Peter wasn't a great dancer. Not embarrassing, but not great. He seemed to know it and made clumsy, self-deprecating remarks in fractured English.

Aisha checked on Christopher, but no, he hadn't moved. He hadn't come looking for her. In fact, he was asking Ms. Baseball to dance.

Fair enough, Aisha told herself. She herself had danced with Peter. Although Peter wasn't quite the dancer Ms. Baseball was.

"So, Peter, what's the deal with you?" Aisha asked. "What are you doing in Vermont?"

"Oh, we are living here now, in Ohio America. I am Russian from Estonia. In Estonia is not good to be Russian. Estonia people don't like us very good."

"So you're like a minority there."

"Yes. Like Negro people in America."

"African-American. Or black. Mostly we don't say Negro."

201

"I offend?"

"No, not at all. I'm the ignorant one. To be honest with you, I don't even know where Estonia is."

He shrugged expressively. "You know where Ohio is, yes? That is my home now."

"So you're just here skiing, like everyone else. Are you any good?"

"Not so good."

Aisha sensed he was just being modest. "How *not so good*?"

He grinned. "I am maybe to be on the Olympic team for America." He waved a hand dismissively. "Probably not."

"No way. That's so cool."

"Very cold, sometimes, yes. You must have proper clothing."

Aisha laughed. "No, I meant *cool* as in—"

But he gave her a wink. "I was making joke. Do you ski?"

"I've taken one lesson." She held up a finger. "I can turn around in a big circle by plopping my skis down one after the other, I can go down a really gentle slope, sometimes even without falling down, and that's it."

"Then I must give you lessons," he said promptly.

"You? I don't think I could exactly afford to pay for an Olympic-level teacher."

"You teach me to dance"—he made a brushing gesture with his two hands—"and we are even."

*　　　*　　　*

"So where do you think Nina and Claire were running off to?" Zoey wondered aloud, taking a long swallow of her drink. She was hot from dancing.

Jake shrugged. "Who knows, with those two? They're the siblings from hell. With Claire and Nina together on this trip, you had to know there'd be bloodshed sooner or later."

"Where's Aisha?" Christopher asked as he returned to the booth. He scanned the dance floor, looking perturbed.

Zoey made a *who knows?* face. "I already lost Lucas in here somewhere." The club was wall-to-wall now, with bodies in motion to the music.

"This place is all right," Jake said into Zoey's ear.

She smiled her agreement. They were getting along, almost like old times. Well, actually, *not* like old times. In the old days they would have been here as a couple, making out, dancing most dances together, holding hands under the table. Now it was like they had begun to be friends again.

And it was all right to talk to old friends, Zoey told herself. About the weather . . . about mutual friends . . . about whether anyone on the football team was using drugs . . .

She made a face. Why did the idea of asking Jake about the story make her feel grubby? It was what reporters did, and if she wanted to be a reporter someday, she'd pretty well have to get used to asking people questions, wouldn't she?

On the other hand, another part of her wanted to write romance novels. It was that part of her that felt uncomfortable using a former boyfriend as a source. Maybe the two careers weren't as compatible as she hoped. Maybe *relentless reporter* and *queen of the love story* didn't go all that well together.

"You know, I'm glad we don't hate each other anymore," Jake said.

Zoey was touched. "I never hated you, Jake."

He nodded. "I know. I was just kidding."

"We're friends, right?" she asked.

He winked. "Absolutely."

Claire came back, as always managing by some magic to make a path through the close-packed bodies, like Moses parting the Red Sea. Nina was behind her, looking abashed and somewhat confused. Zoey saw the two Geiger sisters so often, in such familiar circumstances, that she seldom noticed how much alike they were. But when you saw them together, they looked like . . . well, like sisters, obviously. Both with luxuriant dark hair, though Claire managed to use hers to greater effect; both with startling, almond-shaped eyes, though Nina's were lighter; both with a natural grace that Claire exploited and Nina seemed determined to conceal. Despite Nina's insecurity, Claire wasn't so much more beautiful. And yet the crowd parted for Claire and guys' heads swiveled around to watch her pass, while Nina had to push and shove to keep up.

Claire slid in beside Zoey. Nina sat beside Benjamin and affected an intense interest in what was going on out on the dance floor. She was drumming her fingers and biting her lip.

Suddenly she turned on Benjamin. "So you want to dance, or what?"

"Sure," he said.

"How about you, Claire?" Jake asked, sounding almost timid.

"I'd like to," Claire said neutrally. "But I have to hit the girls' room."

"Be prepared for a major line," Zoey warned her.

The DJ was onto an En Vogue song that Zoey liked and she looked around again for Lucas.

"How about you and me?" Jake said. "I saw Lucas in deep conversation with some guys with purple hair. Snowboarders. You know, you've created a monster getting Lucas into that."

Zoey rolled her eyes. "I'm starting to realize it. That's all he's been talking about." Well, almost all he'd been talking about. She got up and walked with Jake out onto the floor. They danced a fast dance and then, more tentatively, a slow dance.

Holding each other only as close as was proper between friends, Zoey realized she nevertheless felt terribly awkward and uncertain. Not enough time had gone by for her to reach the point where she could touch Jake and feel nothing at all. She wished Lucas were around, but at the same time, she wasn't sure how he would react to seeing her with Jake.

The music had softened enough for conversation. But Zoey's mind was not on chitchat. The time was right. It was now, or maybe not for a long time. And she wanted to at least be able to tell Mr. Schwarz that she had gotten a good start on the story.

"Guess what?" she said brightly.

"What?"

"I got another assignment for a story for the *Weymouth Times.*"

"Cool. I'm proud of you."

"Yeah."

"So what is it? Another story on cafeteria food? I loved that one."

"No, actually, it's kind of a more serious story," she said, feeling a renewed wave of grubbiness at beating around the bush this way.

"Sounds impressive."

"It's about . . . well, I guess there are some rumors about drug use. On the football team."

Jake froze. His hands dropped away from her. His expression grew hard. He shook his head in shock. "Unbelievable."

"It's just a story," Zoey said, talking fast but not fast enough. The damage was done.

"Am I the biggest moron on earth?" Jake demanded bitterly. "I think we're getting back to a point where we're friends, and thinking, okay, this is nice because you know, even if it is over between us, I still really like Zoey. She's a cool girl."

"Look, forget it, Jake. I know *you* probably wouldn't even know if anyone on the team *was* using. I mean, I know you. That's not you at all."

"Nice try, Zoey, but even I'm not *that* dumb." He pushed her away and headed back to the booth, leaving her feeling appalled and ashamed.

Claire had just arrived back from the girls' room. Lucas wandered back and was sipping a drink, giving Jake, and then Zoey a cold, suspicious look.

"I'm out of here," Jake announced.

"I'll go with you," Claire said instantly. She hurried to catch up with him.

"Have a nice time with Jake?" Lucas demanded.

"Not exactly," Zoey said.

Nineteen

"Okay, so we're back in the condo," Benjamin said in a *playing along with a lunatic* tone. "Now can you tell me what this is all about?"

Nina paced the floor of the dark living room, biting her thumb and wondering, quite frankly, what the answer to Benjamin's question was. She had dragged him out onto the dance floor, and then, still feeling edgy and dissatisfied and weirdly excited by Claire's strange confession, she'd dragged him back to the condo. She'd had an image in her mind at the time, something having to do with Claire's injunction to be direct—the queen of manipulation telling her to be direct!—but right now, alone with Benjamin, absolutely alone, no friends, no parents, nothing whatsoever standing between them . . . she had sort of lost the image. Or at least it had become bogged down with frustrating tendrils of reality. The worst of which was Benjamin refusing to play the role she had imagined for him.

Be direct!

"You want to tell me what the hell is the

matter with you, you creep?" she demanded suddenly. Well, it *was* direct.

"The matter with *me*?"

"Yeah. Like . . . like why did you give me all that crap this afternoon? What was that all about?"

Benjamin made a frustrated sound. "Look, you know I don't like people feeling sorry for me."

"I wasn't feeling sorry for you. You twisted scrotal sac."

"Bull. Why were you hanging around here with me, then?"

"How about because I'd rather hang out with you than do anything else?"

Benjamin started to answer, then hesitated. "You're just saying that," he said at last.

"Oh, good retort," Nina said sarcastically.

He pushed his shades back up on his nose and exhaled slowly. "It can't be true that you just really wanted to be with me," he said. "Because, see, if that's true, then I was a real butthole." He shifted his jacket uncomfortably on his shoulders. Then he made a wry smile. "Of course, I don't think I was exactly a *twisted scrotal sac*."

Nina moved closer. He *was* a jerk, maybe, but when he smiled, when he looked at her, near her, in her general direction, whatever was the right phrase for what he did . . . he still made it hard for her to stay mad.

"I thought you were blowing me off," she said. "I thought . . . you know. All that."

"I thought you were, you know, signaling me to back off," he said.

209

"No."

"Me neither."

"Oh. Really?"

"Really."

"*Really?*"

"*Really,*" he said.

"Benjamin . . ."

"Yes?"

"I, uh, I know you're not like in love with me, so don't say you are because I know you aren't, at least not yet, and that's cool." She twisted her fingers together. Be direct. Fine. Direct. "But I really do love you," she blurted in a rush.

He reached toward her. She waited while his hand found her face, stroking her cheek. His fingers touched the tear that had run down it. "Could I kiss you?"

Nina nodded, forgetting, as she sometimes did, that he couldn't see. But he drew her to him, with nothing but the light touch of his gentle fingers trailing down from her cheek to her neck.

This time she had no fears that old memories would come between them. The only memory she had was of their first kiss. And as his lips met hers it was an instant made up of sweetest pleasure and utter relief.

"Let's see if in the future we can't both just say what we're really thinking," Benjamin suggested.

Nina kissed him again.

"You know," she said with a confessional laugh, "I thought Claire set this whole weekend up because she was trying to get you back.

That's why I was so insane tonight."

Benjamin shook his head. "Nah. She set all this up so she could get *Jake* back."

Nina held him out at arm's length. "You *knew* that?"

"Oh, sure. But I let her think I hadn't figured it out." He grinned hugely. "Claire gets such pleasure out of thinking she's outsmarted everyone."

"You're as bad as she is."

"Probably," he admitted. "Maybe that's why even though Claire and I will always have . . . *something* . . . Maybe that's why we both need to have someone nicer and sweeter than ourselves."

"Like me?" Nina asked.

"Exactly like you," Benjamin said. "Except . . . you know, with better taste in music."

Nina kissed him again and drew him slowly down to the couch.

For the second time in the evening, Claire found herself outside the club. Some strange uncontrollable fate seemed to want to keep her out of the warm, welcoming interior and out in the frosty night.

She chased Jake, who was marching forward on his long legs, apparently oblivious to the breeze, which had begun to pick up, cold air tumbling down the slope. She had to run to catch up over ice and snow and between parked cars.

"Hey, wait up!" she called out. "I'll break my neck running after you."

He marched on several paces, but then relented and waited, still staring fixedly ahead.

"Thanks," she said.

He set off again, looking, especially with the steam coming out of his nostrils, like an angry bull.

"You want to tell me what happened between you and Zoey?"

Apparently not. At least not until they were halfway back to the condo, where he stopped so suddenly she ran into him.

"You know, Claire, I have to apologize," he said at last. "I always thought *you* were manipulative."

"Me?" Claire said in a reasonable facsimile of innocent astonishment.

"But I've come to find out Zoey's the one who really plays that game."

"Zoey?" This time it was genuine astonishment.

Jake stopped and turned to face her. "She set me up. I think she set up this whole trip just to loosen me up and get me off my guard."

"Really? Zoey?"

He nodded. He looked grim. "I guess maybe she already told you. I guess you already know about everything."

Claire shook her head cautiously. "I don't think I do, no."

"About my being suspended."

"Suspended . . . from what?"

"From the team."

Claire was shocked. "You were suspended from the team?"

"You didn't know?"

"No. I haven't heard anything about it."

"I wasn't in the game last night. Supposedly I have a pulled hamstring. That's the story. At least until people find out I was skiing over the weekend."

Claire shrugged apologetically. "I don't pay all that much attention to football."

He seemed at least partly relieved. "So maybe it's just Zoey. And the team. And a few others. Zoey probably told Lucas, too. But Lucas doesn't have many friends, so he probably didn't say anything." He started walking again, now at a more reasonable pace, hands deep in his pockets, hunched down inside the collar of his jacket.

"Maybe you could let me in on what's happening," Claire suggested.

He shrugged. "Maybe I should. Maybe you're exactly the person I should tell."

Claire waited patiently, listening to the sound of their footsteps on crisp snow.

"I did up a couple of lines of coke during the homecoming game," he said.

Claire tried to cover her sharp intake of breath by pretending to cough.

"I was hungover and out of it. You saw. I totally blew the first half. Someone . . . no point dragging him into it, but someone said I could do a little coke and straighten up. It worked for a while. We scored some points. Only the coach from the other team wasn't stupid. He told our coach he'd better do something about it. Coach basically told me I could take a piss test right there, and if I was positive I was gone for good from the team. Or—" He made a grim, cynical smile. "I could refuse the test and be suspended until I could take it and pass it. Then Coach covered the whole thing up, told the team to keep quiet." He rolled his eyes. "I pee on Tuesday."

"God, Jake. I had no idea this was going on." There it was again—that unfamiliar feeling of guilt she so disliked. While she had been playing out her clever plan, Jake had been in real, deep trouble. And she hadn't known. In fact, she'd dumped him the day after the team suspended him. Wonderful timing.

"Mmm. Well, Zoey tells me tonight that oh, guess what? She has a story assignment. From the *Weymouth Times*, no less." He waved his hand airily in mimicry of Zoey's nonchalance. "A story about drug use on the team. And oh, by the way, would *I* happen, by any strange coincidence, to know *any*thing about it? Not that *I* would be involved in any way, oh no."

Claire almost burst out laughing, but stifled the urge. The notion of Zoey as ruthless interrogator was just so bizarre. Zoey probably *didn't* know Jake was involved. Knowing Zoey, it would have been a major moral dilemma for her even to bring it up with Jake.

"So you think she arranged this whole trip just to get next to you?" Claire asked.

"Now that I look back. I mean, *she* was the

214

one who invited me. Plus she's been extremely nice to me the whole time."

Claire nodded sagely. She would have liked to clear Zoey of his suspicions, but there wasn't any way to do that without confessing the truth. Oh well, Zoey would survive.

They reached the condo and, by unspoken agreement, stopped outside at the bottom of the deck. "I guess it's not really Zoey I'm mad at, though," Jake said in a low voice. "I'm the one who screwed up. Drinking. Doing coke." He shook his head in disbelief. "I have become a first-class screwup."

Claire stepped closer, not too close, just within the aura of his warmth. "Maybe I had something to do with all of that," she said. "I knew you were feeling, you know, conflicted."

"Nah, it's me. It's me. I can't blame anyone else. No one else forced me to hit the beer as hard as I did. That was me raising the bottles. That was me who let the team down. Me who . . . did other things."

"Everyone makes mistakes," Claire said. "Even the best people. And you are the best, Jake."

Jake bowed his head. "Yeah, I guess everyone does make mistakes. But it's easier to deal with your own mistakes when you haven't been a self-righteous jerk. Telling other people . . . how to live their lives. Refusing ever to forgive . . . other people . . . for the things they did wrong."

Claire held her breath. She hadn't made the connection until that moment. But Jake had.

"I know you didn't mean to—" He struggled to control his voice. "I know it was an accident. You know, with Wade. I just wanted someone to blame. First it was Lucas. Then you. But like you said, *everyone* makes mistakes. Even big dumb straight-arrow jocks like me."

Claire slid her arms around his waist. "You're not so dumb."

"Yeah, I am," he said with feeling. "Any guy who would let you go, no matter what the reason was, is too dumb to believe."

Claire looked up into his eyes. "Jake, I am more sorry than I could ever tell you for what happened with Wade." Her own words, intended only to clinch the moment, suddenly struck home. It occurred to her that she was telling the truth. "There are just two things I deeply regret. One is that I never knew what my uncle was doing to Nina so I could protect her. The other is what I did to you and your family."

She brushed at a tear, amazed to discover it trickling down her cheek.

"I'm freezing," Jake said. "Let's go inside to continue making up. I don't think anyone's back but us."

Claire nodded. "Yes, let's make up for a couple of hours, at least."

Arm in arm, they climbed onto the deck and eased open the sliding glass doors. Claire heard a loud gasp. She turned on the light and saw Nina and Benjamin, clothing rumpled, faces flushed, lying on the couch still wrapped together.

"I'm . . . uh . . . I'm being direct," Nina said, blushing pinker.

"For the first time ever, she does what I tell her to do," Claire said to Jake, shaking her head. "Next I'm going to try telling her to leave home and join a cult."

Twenty

"I'm . . . uh . . . I'm being direct," Nina said, brushing pinker.

"For the first time ever. And does what I tell her to do?" Clea . . . . . ng her head.

"Next I'm going to . . . . to leave home and join a cult."

"People are disappearing around here at an alarming rate," Zoey shouted over the sound of more Aerosmith. "I haven't seen Nina or Benjamin in a while. And now Claire and Jake are both gone, too." She *knew* why Jake was gone, but as to the others . . .

"And I haven't seen Aisha in half an hour now," Christopher said, obviously frustrated.

"Did you piss her off?" Lucas asked.

"No, I didn't piss her off," Christopher said sharply. Then less confidently, "At least, I don't think I pissed her off. We were dancing. Then I happened to hear these people talking about Baltimore, so I got to talking with them about the old hometown and all."

"And these were *guys* from Baltimore?" Lucas asked.

"Some of them were guys. I mean, there was one dude. But it's not what you're thinking. They weren't even all that cool-looking or anything. The one was a total head-bag situation."

"I'm sure I didn't really hear you say that,"

Zoey said, shooting Christopher a withering look.

"Personally, I don't approve of that kind of sexist talk," Lucas said. He put his arm around Zoey. "I'm much too enlightened."

"I'm going to go look for her some more," Christopher said. "Maybe she went back to the condo." He got up and melted into the crowd.

"Great, now everyone will be back at the condo," Lucas said darkly. "No privacy at all for us. What if we want to discuss the meaning of life?"

"I'll bet that's just what you want to discuss," Zoey said. But Lucas was right. The condo would be way too crowded for Zoey to have to worry about anything happening. Which was especially good, because after the disastrous encounter with Jake, romance was about the last thing on her mind.

Lucas looked disappointed, almost glum. Then a light came on in his eyes. "So you want to get out of here?"

"Shouldn't we wait for Christopher and Eesh?"

"They're semi-adults. They can find their own way back."

They got up and walked out into the night. As they neared the condo they heard a strange, compelling sound—a brilliant soprano voice soaring from one impossibly high note to the next.

"I'm guessing that's Benjamin," Lucas said.

Zoey grinned. "No, Benjamin's a tenor."

They found Benjamin with Nina in the hot tub, the portable CD player belting out opera.

"Quick, Zoey," Lucas said. "The pod people have taken control of Nina."

Nina splashed a handful of water toward him, missing. "Hey, shut up, this is my favorite *area*."

"Aria," Benjamin corrected.

"Are I *what*?" Nina came back, laughing in appreciation of her own wit.

"No, that's not a pod," Lucas admitted. "It's still Nina."

Zoey pulled him away. "I don't think they want *us* hanging around," she whispered.

"Oh, yeah. Look, um, where are your keys to the van? I sort of left something out there."

Zoey found her purse and Lucas hurried away, looking like a naughty child planning a prank. She went upstairs and found one bedroom door closed. She considered knocking, but decided against it. From inside there were indistinct, low murmuring sounds that didn't sound like an invitation.

She went into the other bedroom and flopped back on a bed. The bed was slated to be either Lucas's or Jake's. She didn't much care, since neither of them was around. She wondered what was going on in the next room. Obviously it had to be Jake and Claire. Unless, by some weird twist of fate, it was Jake and Aisha. That seemed pretty unlikely, but then, unlikely things had become commonplace lately, ever since Lucas had returned to Chatham Island and she and Jake had broken up. It really wasn't all that strange that Jake and Claire would be back together, having just broken up exactly a week earlier.

Lucas was in the doorway. "That's *Jake's* bed, you know."

Zoey shrugged. "I was tired. I flopped on the first soft flat surface I saw."

"Well, uh, look, I have a kind of surprise for you."

"A surprise?" She tried to sound excited, but she really was weary. The run-in with Jake had punctured her good mood. Jake thought she was ruthless enough to try to use him for her own selfish reasons. And he wasn't far from being right.

"Come on." Lucas took her hand and pulled her to her feet. As often happened, his touch revived her, at least a little. She slipped her arms around him and gave him a kiss.

"Not here," Lucas said conspiratorially. "Any second now Nina or Aisha or Claire or someone will come barging in."

"You have a better place?"

"Ha. It happens I do."

He kept her hand in his and led her swiftly down the stairs and out the front door to the parking lot. The van was running, exhaust billowing.

Lucas opened the side door, climbed in, and drew her after him. He'd had the heat running and it was perfectly warm. The seats had been reconfigured to make a little open area, just big enough for the two of them to lie side by side on the unzipped sleeping bag he'd laid out.

Zoey laughed appreciatively. "You went to a lot of trouble."

"Nothing but the best for you," he said. "At least it's private."

"Except for the windows."

"We'll just have to steam those up," he said.

With some reluctance, Aisha had accepted Peter's offer to run over to his hotel for a minute. First, she barely knew the guy. Second, she couldn't find Christopher to tell him she was leaving. Third, it was the kind of thing that Christopher, with his one-track mind, might misinterpret.

On the other hand, she'd reminded herself, when last seen, Christopher had been dancing with Ms. Baseball and keeping a very close eye on her every move. And Peter seemed like a nice enough guy. What were the odds he was a crazed Estonian ax murderer? But in case he was, she decided maybe she'd just wait in the lobby.

They had spent their time sitting on the overstuffed lobby chairs, looking through a small photo album he had. Pictures of Mom and Dad. Pictures of his three sisters. Pictures of the old home back in Estonia that brought tears to his eyes. Pictures of the new home in Ohio.

That was it. No ax murdering. Not even an attempt to kiss her. He was just a sweet, polite guy who'd wanted her to have a cup of hot tea with him and look at pictures of the old, lost homestead.

Then, when she'd begun to yawn, he'd insisted on walking her back to the condo.

As they walked, it was impossible for Aisha

not to compare Peter with Christopher. One gentle, the other brash. One modest, the other with half the world's supply of ego. Peter even had a girlfriend back in Estonia that he had been faithful to until she had written him to say she was dating a bus driver.

He didn't have the effect on her that Christopher had, didn't make her want to kiss him the way Christopher did. Didn't make her feel crazy the way Christopher always had and probably always would. But he was nice. It was like a reminder that nice, cute, gentle, sweet guys (who, if they skied competitively, probably had bodies like steel) were still out there in the world.

In other words, there was a world beyond Christopher.

The condo was dark and Aisha realized, with a shocked look at her watch, that it was very late. The moon had set and there was no sound except for a car engine idling in the parking lot.

"I had fun, Peter."

"I like you very much," Peter said.

"Maybe I'll see you tomorrow."

"Please, yes."

To her surprise he leaned close and gave her a chaste peck on the cheek. "Good night, Aisha."

"Night." She climbed the steps to the deck as quietly as she could. Maybe she could get through the living room and upstairs without waking anyone up. But before she could put her hand on the sliding glass door, it opened.

"Where *the hell* have you been?"

Christopher. "Sorry, I hope I didn't worry anyone," Aisha whispered. "I kind of lost track of time."

"Why should I worry just because you disappear for hours and turn up with some guy who kisses you right out there in front of me?"

"Like I said, I'm sorry. But you're not my father, all right?"

"Where did you go with him?" Christopher demanded.

Aisha pushed past him into the warmth of the living room. In the dark she sensed another person, but peering around, she could see no one. Christopher was still fully dressed. Obviously he had been waiting up for her, no doubt fuming the entire time.

Well, well. So *he* was jealous.

"I went to his hotel room to look at some things he wanted to show me," Aisha said. Yes, she could have chosen her words a little more carefully, but why not let Christopher imagine the worst?

"You . . . You . . . to his . . ." Christopher sputtered. "Just what did he show you?"

"Is there someone else in here?" Aisha asked.

"Benjamin's on the floor," Christopher said. "He's asleep."

"Yeah," a voice said, "and I can't hear a thing."

"Look, don't try and change the subject," Christopher said angrily.

"Fine. Same subject. What were you and the Baltimore Areolas talking about?"

"Can you clarify that?" Benjamin asked.

224

"Some girl wearing a Baltimore Orioles T-shirt," Aisha said.

Benjamin chuckled. "That's pretty good, Aisha."

"Thanks."

"Okay, fine," Christopher said. "You don't want to tell me, cool. You don't have to."

"Good," Aisha said brightly. "Good night."

"Wait! Where are you going?"

"Up to bed."

"You really *aren't* going to tell me what you did with that dude? Don't you think I have a right to know? Don't you think you owe me some honesty?"

Aisha smiled contentedly as she climbed the stairs. Sometimes life just worked out so well.

Twenty-one

The van windows had been well steamed.

They had made out for what seemed to Zoey a long time. Not that she was complaining. Only it didn't seem like Lucas was getting tired, and she was.

"Maybe we should go inside," she suggested.

"Too many people in there," he said. He kissed the hollow of her neck, something that never failed to send shivers through her.

"Mmmm. Yes. Only, look, we have to get some sleep."

"Do we? I'm not tired."

She shoved him playfully. "You're never tired. You're the Energizer Bunny when it comes to making out."

"Don't you like it?" he asked.

"Of course I like it. Have I been acting like I don't?"

He shook his head. "No. But see, I don't want to go to sleep. I . . . look, Zoey. I want to make love. I even bought condoms because last time you said it was rotten of me even to suggest it unless we were protected and all." He

226

fumbled around in the corner behind the front seat and pulled out a string of condoms, holding them up as evidence.

Zoey recoiled, scooting back away from him. Then, realizing how ridiculous her reaction had been, she started giggling.

"I don't think this is funny," Lucas said.

But Zoey couldn't stop now. She was giggling herself into hiccups.

"Damn it, Zoey," Lucas said sharply. "Don't laugh at me."

Obviously his feelings had been hurt, but still Zoey couldn't stop laughing. She was beginning to get alarmed.

He touched her, but she shook off his hand. He sat back, his eyes furious. At last Zoey got the spasms of laughter under control.

"I'm sorry," she said in a choked voice. "I wasn't laughing at you, Lucas."

"Yeah, it's real funny that I love you, isn't it? Big laugh."

"Lucas, that's not it," Zoey said. "I was just . . . I don't know, I was tense or something. It's been kind of a bad night. Jake and I—"

"*Jake?* What about Jake?"

"Nothing, nothing." She waved a dismissive hand.

"Look, Zoey, we're here together, we're alone, your mom or dad isn't suddenly going to show up . . . I mean, if we're not going to do it now, when are we going to?"

Zoey felt a wave of weariness mixed with

frustration sweep over her. This day had started with the nerve-wracking drive, followed by arguments over beds, followed by too much skiing on out-of-shape muscles, followed by having Jake make her feel like a jerk. The best part had been the last hour, here with Lucas. Only now he seemed determined to ruin even that.

"Lucas, I told you. I don't know. I love you. I think you're amazingly hot. But I'm not ready yet to start having sex."

"Why? Can you just tell me that? Why?"

"Lucas, look, I've thought about this lately. I've been thinking about it a lot. I know a lot of people our age are doing it and all, and I know *you* want to. But, see, the thing is, I used to think about doing it with Jake, too, back when we were together. He used to be the one asking, and I was saying no. If I had slept with him, and then we'd broken up the way we did . . . I mean, it's not like it's just going to be one time, with one person. You think it will be, but if I'd slept with Jake, and then with you, that would be two guys right there, and I'm only seventeen."

"So I'm nothing more to you than Jake was," he said coldly.

"That's not what I'm saying," she protested. "But okay, how about this? If we slept together tonight, what about tomorrow night? What about every night from now on? It's not like you'd get tired of doing it. It would take over our lives. That's all our relationship would be about."

"You know, it is at least *slightly* possible that

you might enjoy it, too," Lucas said.

"It's very possible," Zoey said softly. "Of course I would. Of course I'd enjoy being closer to you than I've ever been with anyone else, Lucas. I enjoy *everything* we do together, even the things where I tell you to stop. But whether I enjoy something isn't the only thing to consider. You're not the one who has to worry about getting pregnant, for example."

"I would always stand by you if something like that happened," he said fiercely.

"Oh, Lucas, see? That's what I mean. It's not something *you* have to think about as seriously as I do. First of all, if I got pregnant and *if* I decided to have the baby, are you going to support us? And pay for a baby-sitter so I can still go to college? On what? Minimum wage?"

He nodded slowly, but not as a sign of agreement. "In other words, we will never have sex."

"I'm not saying that."

"Then when? Give me a date or a time or something. The turn of the millennium? Next time Halley's Comet passes by? When? I mean, I thought when we decided to do this little weekend trip, that meant you were ready to be more grown up."

"I never said that. I never promised you; in fact I told you just the opposite."

"Fine. Not tonight, then. Tomorrow night? When?"

Zoey buried her face in her hands. "Damn it, Lucas."

"When?"

Her self-control snapped. "When I'm ready, that's when," she spat. "When *I* say that *I'm* ready."

"You know something, Zoey? Screw you."

"Lucas . . ."

"You're a very smart girl. You can come up with a million reasons why you don't want to make love to me. But I'm not going to wait around to hear them all. See, the hard fact is, I don't have to wait for you to make up your mind. If it's not you, then it will be someone else, Zoey. When you decide you're ready, you let me know. I *may* still care."

He slid open the van door, jumped out, and slammed it shut violently behind him. The inside of the van rang with the silence. Zoey slumped against the side wall and drew the sleeping bag up around her. She felt stunned, too stunned to think or analyze. It had all happened so suddenly. One minute they were bantering, the next kissing, and in an instant, *an instant,* it was all over.

All over with the guy she loved with all her heart.

Twenty-two

It was almost morning before Zoey got out of the van. She'd had to turn off the engine for fear of getting gassed by the exhaust, and after that the temperature inside had dropped dramatically.

She had spent hours, sometimes crying, sometimes imagining one scenario after another—Lucas would come out and say he was sorry, that he hadn't meant it, that it was all some male equivalent of PMS. Or, alternately, she would go to him, crawl into his warm bed, and make love to him so gently and quietly that no one else in the room would even know.

But she knew neither scenario was going to happen. And after a while she cried no more, just stared blankly, feeling drained of all energy, grim, and utterly depressed.

As she stretched her cramped limbs and climbed out of the van, the stars were still visible in the sky, but the mountains could now be seen as darker masses against a somewhat lighter sky. Soon the sun would begin peeking through the valleys, and Zoey wanted to be gone before then.

She went into the condo, grateful for the

warmth. Christopher was breathing heavily, sprawled in a dream across the couch. Benjamin was rolled tightly in a sleeping bag on the floor. As silently as she could, she went to Benjamin and knelt beside him. She could hear the pattern of his breathing change. He knew she was there.

"Hi," she whispered.

"What's up?"

"Look, um, I've decided to go home early. They have a bus that runs from the village. It's not that expensive or anything."

In the gloom she could see his blank eyes searching, as though they might somehow see something. "What's the matter?"

"It's too complicated to go into, Benjamin."

"Oh. You and Lucas break up or something?"

"Something. I guess we did break up." Even now she couldn't keep the quiver out of her voice.

"I'm sorry, kid," he whispered. He found her and gave her a hug. "You don't have to leave, though."

She sighed deeply. "Lucas hates me. Jake hates me over something else. It wouldn't be any fun for me or for them."

"I still like you," Benjamin said.

"You're my big brother. You have to." She pressed the keys to the van into his hand. "Tell everyone to stay and have fun. Especially you and Nina. Okay? I'll be fine. And make sure you get my skis home."

She hugged him tightly again and got up to go, feeling more alone than she had ever felt before.

232

Claire

Jake would say yes, yes, and yes. But then, Jake is a romantic. I don't like trying to guess the future— it never, ever works. Which is why life is interesting.

Aisha

If he's honest, I'm afraid he'd answer yes, yes, and no. I guess I'd rather it was either three straight yeses or three straight no's. I'd like to just know, one way or the other, so I could concentrate on more important things.

Nina

Benjamin would answer who knows? who knows? and who knows? For my answer I would have to call the Psychic Friends Network.

Zoey

~~I know Lucas and I feel the same about this yes, yes, and yes.~~

Twenty-three

The bus ride took forever. Killington to Boston, then a change of buses to go to Portland and a second change to get back to Weymouth. On the ride she slept a little and cried some more, hoping with what energy she could muster that Lucas would bitterly regret being such a jerk.

It was late afternoon before she caught the familiar ferry and saw the comforting silhouette of Chatham Island approaching. She was exhausted beyond belief, caught in an endless, gray dream of remembered conversations, secret wishes, and resilient hopes that clung to life despite everything.

She got off the ferry and briefly considered stopping in at the restaurant. But at this time of day her father would be in the kitchen and her mother would be at home, sleeping in preparation for the Sunday night bar shift. Showing up back home a day early would just worry her father. This was more a mother-daughter type of thing.

She slogged through the streets and almost collapsed with relief on reaching her home. A good, long night of sleep and the events of the trip would all seem much clearer. Maybe Lucas would call and say all the things she still desperately hoped he would say. Maybe he had already caught the next bus and was on his way to her. Maybe.

She went in quietly, not wanting to wake her mother earlier than necessary. She dropped her bag at the foot of the stairs and made her way up.

At the top landing she heard a sound. Her mother's voice, a low murmur.

She went to her parents' bedroom door. It was open several inches.

"Mom?"

She heard a muttered curse. A rapid shuffling, another curse, this time a man's voice. A figure flashed past the open door. Running, pulling on a shirt in a frantic rush. A man.

A man, not her father.

Not *her* father.

But a man she had recognized beyond a shadow of a doubt.